"I Guess We Should Talk About Money,"

Stone said.

Allison laughed a little, confused. "Wait a minute. I'm not sure—"

"So do you charge by the hour or what?"

Allison blinked. "Well, generally we charge by the job, though there are certain set fees...."

He nodded. "Of course."

"But since we really haven't talked about what you want..."

He looked a little uncomfortable. "I told you, nothing personal. Not that I don't think you're attractive—I do—and not that I wouldn't like to—well, of course I would—but let's just keep it business for now, okay? Just the wedding. How much?"

A dull ache of recognition was pushing at the back of Allison's mind, and she absolutely refused to acknowledge it. She said carefully, "For *what?*"

Dear Reader,

Welcome to Silhouette Desire! The fabulous things we have to offer you in Silhouette Desire just keep on coming. October is simply chock-full of delicious goodies to keep even the most picky romance reader happy all month long.

First, we have a thrilling new *Man of the Month* book from talented author Paula Detmer Riggs. It's called *A Man of Honor,* and I know Max Kaler is a hero you'll never forget.

Next, Annette Broadrick's SONS OF TEXAS series continues with *Courtship Texas Style!* Please *don't* worry if you didn't catch the beginning of this series, because each of the SONS OF TEXAS stands alone (and how!).

For those of you who are Lass Small fans—and you all know who you are!—her connecting series about those FABULOUS BROWN BROTHERS continues with *Two Halves.* Again, please don't fret if you haven't read about the *other* Brown Brothers, because Mike Brown is a hero in his own right!

I'm always thrilled to be able to introduce new authors to the Silhouette Desire family, and Anne Marie Winston is someone you'll be seeing a lot of in the future. Her first published book ever, *Best Kept Secrets,* is highlighted this month as a PREMIERE title. Watch for future Desire books by this talented newcomer in Spring 1993.

This month is completed in a most delightful way with Jackie Merritt's *Black Creek Ranch* (a new book by Jackie is always a thrill) and Donna Carlisle's *It's Only Make Believe.*

As for November . . . well, I'd tell you all about it, but I've run out of space. You'll just have to wait!

So until next month, happy reading,

Lucia Macro
Senior Editor

DONNA CARLISLE

IT'S ONLY MAKE BELIEVE

SILHOUETTE *Desire*

Published by Silhouette Books New York

America's Publisher of Contemporary Romance

SILHOUETTE BOOKS
300 East 42nd St., New York, N.Y. 10017

IT'S ONLY MAKE BELIEVE

ISBN: 0-373-05741-5

First Silhouette Books printing October 1992

Books by Donna Carlisle

Silhouette Desire

Under Cover #417
A Man Around the House #476
Interlude #530
Matchmaker, Matchmaker #555
For Keeps #634
The Stormriders #681
Cast Adrift #700
It's Only Make Believe #741

DONNA CARLISLE

lives in Atlanta, Georgia, with her teenage daughter. Weekends and summers are spent in her rustic north Georgia cabin, where she enjoys hiking, painting and planning her next novel.

Donna has also written under the pseudonyms Rebecca Flanders and Leigh Bristol.

One

Allison frowned distractedly and did not look up from the computer screen as she said, "What did you say his name was?"

"Stone," Penny replied. "Stone Harrison."

That got Allison's attention, and she stared at her partner. "Are you sure you heard him right?"

Penny tossed Allison an impatient look as she hurried around the small office, gathering files and ledgers and other miscellaneous scraps of paper and stuffing them into her briefcase. "Come on, Allison, this is serious. Are you almost ready with that printout?"

"What kind of name is *Stone?*" Allison tapped the function key on the computer a couple of times, as though doing so might change the numbers on the screen into something more to her liking. It did not, and she sighed. "Take my advice and go without it."

Penny glanced at her anxiously. "That bad, huh?"

"Believe me, you don't want to know."

Penny looked uncertain for a moment, then squared her shoulders. "Well, don't worry. I'm sure Harry will figure out some clever way to get us through. He always does."

Harry was their accountant, and he had proven his cleverness more than once in the three years Party Girls had been in business. But Allison secretly doubted even Harry would be able to pull another miracle out of his hat—and a miracle was exactly what it was going to take to keep the business afloat for another quarter.

She murmured morosely, "Maybe he can loan us the money to pay our taxes." She hit the Save button on the computer and the screen went gray.

"That's exactly," Penny told her, snapping her briefcase closed, "why it's so important that we get this job from Mr. Harrison."

"But why do I have to do it?" Allison insisted. "You know I make a rotten first impression. You're the front man in this operation. You charm the clients, I do the work, that was the deal. If this guy really is important, the last thing you want to do is turn me loose on him."

Penny looked a little worried about that herself as she flipped her hair from beneath the collar of her blazer and gave her reflection a brief inspection in the mirror over the credenza. Penny was a former fashion model and a past Miss California, both of which were assets that still served her well—and which she still did her best to cultivate. "You know I would if I didn't have to be at the dentist's the minute I get finished with Harry. Besides . . ." She forced confidence into her tone along with a bright smile. "You'll do fine, I know you will."

Allison suggested hopefully, "Why don't *I* meet with Harry and have my teeth cleaned while *you* keep the appointment with Mr. Harrison?"

"Now you're just trying to be difficult. You know it's going to take both of us out there hustling clients to get through this recession and you need the practice."

"The last time I practiced," Allison reminded her darkly, "we ended up catering an eighteen-thousand-dollar wedding for eight thousand dollars."

"I *still* don't understand how that happened," Penny admitted. "You're so organized in the office..."

"And the time before that we almost ended up in a lawsuit—"

"You just can't let them fluster you," Penny insisted. "You've got to keep telling yourself that our clients are just ordinary people, and stop letting them intimidate you."

Allison propped her chin up on her hands and responded dryly, "Ordinary people do not fill their swimming pools with orchids or cater candlelit dinners for two on top of mountains that are accessible only by helicopter. Our clients are rich, spoiled and weird. There's nothing ordinary about them and I've got a perfect right to be intimidated."

"Well..." Penny gave her hair a final pat and picked up her briefcase. "Just try not to let them intimidate you out of any money, okay? Besides, Mr. Harrison is perfectly normal, I promise."

"Oh, yeah? Then where did he get a name like Stone?"

"I hardly think that's any of your business." She shot Allison a warning look. "And don't you dare ask him."

"What does he do for a living?"

"I'm not sure. Something about building castles I think."

Penny paused on her way out the door, looked as though she would like to explain that, then thought better of it or—more likely—didn't have an explanation. She said instead, "Just be nice...and be careful." She hurried out the door.

"Castles," repeated Allison dully to the empty room. "Why not?"

The headquarters of Party Girls was actually the living room of Allison's Los Angeles town house. Its inventory consisted of a stack of letterhead, a personal computer and an answering machine—all of which saved on overhead considerably. *Save* had become a key word in Allison's vocabulary over the past year or so.

The idea for an exclusive party planning and catering service had been Allison's; the name Party Girls had been Penny's idea and they still argued over that sometimes. At the time it had seemed to be the perfect business venture: with Allison's business skills and Penny's socialite contacts—her father had been a diplomat and her ex-husband a record producer, which gave her a Rolodex filled with jet-setters and blue bloods—it seemed like a match made in heaven. Los Angeles and environs was an area brimming with elegance, eccentrics and money, and Party Girls was an idea whose time had come...almost.

Almost was, unfortunately, the story of Allison's life. She had almost gotten a degree in film making,

just as she had almost gotten a degree in art history.
She had almost gone to Europe with an impulsive, incredibly eccentric artist with whom she was almost in
love. She had almost gotten an executive trainee position with one of the fastest-growing new businesses
in Canada—vice presidency guaranteed within five
years—and when she had missed that one by inches
she had decided to stop waiting for some outside force
to change her life and start making the good things
happen herself. That was when she remembered how
many friends had asked her to help plan their weddings, their dinner parties, their romantic weekends,
and that was when she had been struck by the *almost
perfect* idea for Party Girls.

Or at least that was how she liked to remember the
idea had come about. The truth was she and Penny
had been sitting around one evening, a bottle of wine
between them, feeling sorry for themselves—Penny
because of her divorce, Allison because of her almost
perpetual state of unemployment—and they had begun listing their assets: Allison had the rented town
house she could hardly afford, Penny had her ali-
mony. Allison had an eclectic educational background and a flair for understanding the nuances that
made a social occasion a success or failure, and Penny
had an address book full of private, unlisted phone
numbers. Allison was a gourmet cook, Penny an au-
thority on wine. They were both desperate for a job
and ready to try anything.

Several things had conspired to make Allison's first
venture into the world of business a near-miss success. Ten years ago the success of a business such as
Party Girls would have been assured, but people were
more careful with their money these days. Prudence,

not indulgence, was the byword of the times, and eccentric millionaires were getting harder and harder to find. Allison hated dealing with clients and she wasn't very good at it, which was why she had Penny. But try as she might, Penny could not scale down her imagination to plan an ordinary wedding for ordinary people within an ordinary budget. Horse-drawn carriages and white doves inevitably entered into the picture with skyrocketing expenses, which effectively eliminated the workaday segment of the population that might have supported them through hard times.

Furthermore, Party Girls was a rotten name for a business. Allison could take the blame for the idea, the timing and, even to some extent, the clients, but only Penny was responsible for the name.

Allison picked up the business card Penny had left on the desk and turned it over, frowning. Speaking of names... Stone Harrison. *Stone.* What kind of name was that? Perfectly appropriate for someone who built castles she supposed.

And suddenly she sat up straight, staring at the door by which her partner had left in such a rush. Penny had forgotten to tell her *what* kind of party Mr. Stone Harrison wanted. A wedding, a birthday, a welcome home, bon voyage, congratulations, no reason at all... There were as many parties as there were occasions— no, more—and how was she supposed to give him a sales pitch if she didn't even know why he had called?

"Great," she muttered. "Thanks a lot, Penny." She only hoped that Mr. Harrison had not been planning on spending a lot of money, because she always felt worse about losing big jobs than small ones.

With an air of weary martyrdom she checked the address on the card again and picked up her jacket and her purse. Castles, indeed.

"Carla!" Stone bellowed, slamming down the telephone receiver. He pushed the intercom button and shouted into it again, "Carla!" When that produced no response after two seconds he stood up and yelled, "Car-la!"

His secretary appeared at the door to his office, unhurried, unruffled, one eyebrow raised coolly. "Your Highness?"

Scowling, Stone gripped his forehead with both hands and demanded, "Aspirin!"

Her look changed from one of superior disdain to a kind of smug sympathy. "No luck, huh?"

Stone paced to the window and stabbed the button that opened the floor-length black shutter, glaring down at a picture-perfect Southern California autumn day, which wasn't much different from a perfect Southern California summer day. "I'm thirty-two years old," he announced, "free of disease and bad habits, brilliant, self-employed, moderately wealthy, passably good-looking—"

"Well groomed," Carla put in helpfully. "A snappy dresser."

He gave a short nod of agreement. "So why is it that a man with those qualifications can't find one woman in this entire city to go out with him?"

"Well," began Carla, with perhaps a trifle too much enthusiasm.

"It's not as though I was asking them to take a ride on the space shuttle! One little wedding—"

"For heaven's sake, Stone, you don't just ask a woman to a formal wedding on twenty-four-hours notice! Particularly not your ex-wife's wedding!"

He turned on her, demanding in all innocence, "Why not?" Then, hopefully, "Say, Carla, what are you doing tomorrow night?"

She gave him her most forbidding frown. "Washing my hair."

"Could you—"

"With my husband."

He let his shoulders slump in defeat, turning back to the window. "It's all Susan's fault, you know. What kind of woman would break up a perfectly good relationship for no reason at all, two days before I have to attend a wedding?" He turned back to her, his tone accusing. "You're a woman. Explain *that* to me if you can."

"Oh, I don't know. It couldn't have anything to do with the fact that you broke more dates with her than you kept—most of the time without even bothering to call. That you forgot her birthday. That you forgot *Christmas.* That you left her parents standing in the rain after promising to pick them up at the station—"

"Hey, that wasn't my fault," Stone objected, although he did have the good grace to look abashed. "You were supposed to remind me."

"That you are in general selfish, inconsiderate, demanding and, frankly, more than a little spoiled. Why, other than that, Stone Harrison, I can't think of a reason in the world why any woman in her right mind would ever think she could live without you."

Stone frowned uncomfortably. "I'm not spoiled," he muttered.

He pushed his fingers through his hair, letting the frown deepen as he released a long breath. "This couldn't have happened at a worse time. Susan knew how much I was counting on her to get me through the next month while the Japanese are here..."

"Now you're talking about something I can do something about. When it comes to social entertaining, you're hopeless—with or without Susan. You're going to have to hire those consultants I told you about—"

"You know how much that contract means to me," Stone went on, not listening. "And you know how much I hate all that wining and dining I'm going to have to do to get it. Why do the two have to be related, anyway, will you tell me that? At least with a woman along you have somebody to look at between courses—which is why, in my opinion, most men get married."

"I'll be sure to register your opinion if anyone ever asks," Carla returned pertly. "But in the meantime you're left with an awful lot of entertaining to do and no hostess—which, I might add, is the least of your problems."

Ignoring the last part of her observation, Stone adamantly agreed with the first. "Right. And you call *me* inconsiderate? What do you say about a woman who'd leave me in this kind of lurch?"

The outer office door chime sounded, announcing a visitor. Carla gave Stone a dry look as she said, "Yes. It's too bad Susan couldn't have arranged her broken heart for a more convenient time, isn't it?"

Stone didn't know how to reply to that, and he was disturbed, but only for a moment. Susan's heart had not been broken any more than his was. He had never had a relationship in his life that was intense enough to cause heartbreak on either side—and that included his marriage. He suspected that Susan, as he, was more than a little relieved to have it over with. In a few months they'd be having lunch together and looking back wistfully on the time they had shared, which was exactly how every relationship he had ever had with a woman eventually ended up.

In the meantime, he still had a problem.

"Maybe my mother," he mumbled. But his mother already had a date for the wedding.

Stone Harrison was good at a great many things; however, managing the small complications of life like keeping appointments, making reservations, and maintaining relationships were not among them. His mother used to accuse him of living with only one foot in the real world and that was part of it, he supposed. But if Stone were strictly honest with himself, which he tried to be whenever it wasn't too inconvenient, he would have to admit that a greater part of his inability to manage his personal life with any noticeable amount of success was sheer disinterest.

He simply wasn't accustomed to dealing with so many complications at once. The Heroshito contract was consuming him day and night. He had worked harder on it and wanted it more than anything else in his life. The possibility of a late-breaking complication in his personal life was something he simply was not prepared for, and if left to his own devices, he would have preferred to ignore it altogether and bury himself in his work. He did not, unfortunately, have that luxury. Everyone he knew was going to be at Melinda's wedding. His own *mother* was going to be there. He had always felt that his ex-wife took far too personal an interest in how he was managing without her. If he showed up without a date...

He rubbed his temples. The headache he had feigned for Carla was starting to turn into the real thing. Maybe it would develop into a full-blown migraine and he wouldn't have to go to the wedding.

A light tap on his door startled Stone. Carla never knocked unless she was introducing a visitor and Stone wasn't expecting anyone. But then he didn't recall having looked at his appointment calendar that day.

Sure enough, Carla came in, escorting a young woman with a briefcase. "Mr. Harrison," she said in her perfect-secretary voice, "this is Allison Carter, from Party Girls." And when Stone looked at her blankly, she pressed a business card into his hand and winked at him. "The solution to all your problems," she assured him.

It took Stone a moment to understand, and another moment to believe it. As the door closed on Carla's exit, he looked from the business card in his hand to the woman standing across from him. *Party Girls.* Carla's idea of a joke?

The woman extended her hand in a very business-like fashion. "Mr. Harrison," she said. "It's a pleasure to meet you."

And that was when he realized it wasn't a joke at all. It might actually *be* the solution to all his problems.

Her hand was small and feminine, but her grip firm. That surprised him for some reason. In fact, all of her surprised him, which he supposed served him right for trying to stereotype people. She was wearing a short black pleated skirt and a long red jacket, dark stockings, moderate heels, stylish but conservative. Her briefcase appeared to be leather and had her initials discreetly engraved in script on the clasp. Her blond-brown hair was worn in a very ordinary style, cut just below the ears and pushed back from her face with a tortoiseshell hair band. Her figure appeared to be good, but not perfect—certainly not voluptuous. She was…cute. If Stone had to sum up her appearance in one word, that would be it. Cute. And not at all what he would have expected under the circumstances.

Those circumstances might have thrown another man off balance, but if there was one thing Stone excelled at it was adapting to the unexpected, seizing the moment, turning the bizarre into the advantageous. This situation would definitely have to be classified bizarre, but it took him only a moment to see the advantages, and only another moment to wonder why he hadn't thought of it himself. He needed a date for the wedding, a hostess for his clients, an escort. A woman. And Carla, with her typical expertise, had brought forth the only possible solution—hire a professional.

He realized he had been staring at her in an almost bemused fashion, and that his silence was on the edge of becoming awkward. He said quickly, "Well, Miss…" He glanced at the card. "Carter. Come in, won't you? Have a seat."

All the way to Harrison's office Allison had been reciting to herself the reasons she hated dealing with clients, but not until she came face-to-face with Stone Harrison did any of those reasons seem to have any relevance. She knew that there was something about her appearance that seemed to prohibit people from taking her seriously. She had been called *cute* more times than she cared to recall and that was her first handicap. She was also accustomed to men's lingering assessive gazes—though she couldn't recall the last time any gaze had been quite so lingering, or quite so assessive as Stone Harrison's was now—and had learned to accept them as part of the job. What she wasn't accustomed to was being stopped in her tracks by a man, particularly by a client.

Thanks to Penny, and the eccentric nature of the business, she had met her share of characters, of near-celebrities, of movers and shakers, of the idle rich. Quite a few were men. Some were even as good-looking as—if not better than—Stone Harrison. All of them she found incredibly easy to resist, but Stone Harrison caught her off guard. He was not what she had expected at all.

His office was on the sixth floor of a downtown bank building. The reception area was upscale elegant; his private office was chrome and smoked glass and high-tech black and gray. Stone lounged in faded jeans and a black sweatshirt, with rumpled brown hair and a faintly stubbled jaw and the most extraordinary, sexy-soft bedroom-gray eyes that Allison had ever seen. Those eyes were framed by a pair of dark brows and surrounded by eyelashes so thick they formed a smudge, like an artistic smear of charcoal, accenting his eyes. Perhaps that was what made his eyes look as though they could see into another world. They looked at Allison and made her wish, for a ridiculous moment, that they would never look away.

He was attractive, yes. He was surprising, certainly. But more than that, he was likable; Allison could tell that immediately. Before he'd said a word she knew he was the most interesting man she had ever met—and this from a woman who had once almost run away to Europe to live with an artist. *That* was what caught her off guard and, that was why for what seemed to be an embarrassingly long interval after looking into his eyes, Allison couldn't seem to remember why she was there.

She took the leather-and-chrome sling chair he indicated and cleared her throat a little, gathering her thoughts. He was a client, she reminded herself. More interesting than most but a client nonetheless, and she had promised Penny she would try to do this right. The sign on the door said Stonewall Enterprises, Gregory S. Harrison, Pres. and, whatever else Stone Harrison might be, if he could afford these offices he had to have money.

She gave him her most charming smile and said, "You'll have to forgive me, Mr. Harrison, but I'm afraid I'm not entirely prepared. What kind of party did you have in mind?"

He stared at her. "Maybe I should ask," he suggested slowly, "what you offer."

And just as Allison opened her mouth to do so, he lifted a hand in protest, as though censoring his own thoughts, and said quickly, "No. Never mind. Listen, this is…" He grinned and spread his hands. It was the most disarming gesture Allison had ever seen. "Believe it or not this is the first time I've ever done anything like this. It's a little awkward for me."

He had a young face—not boyish, but youthful, open, adventurous. When he grinned a spark came into his eyes that danced on the edge of wickedness and made Allison want to grin back without even knowing why.

She said in her warmest professional voice, "I understand. But there's really nothing to be uncomfortable about. A lot of people need help for one reason or another and that's what Party Girls is here for. We specialize in exactly what you need.''

He gave her another one of those odd looks that was a cross between a nonplussed stare and frank, almost probing, curiosity, and he said, ''How do you know what I need?'' But once again he raised a hand to forestall her reply. ''Don't answer that. I don't think we should be having this conversation during business hours.''

''If another time would be more convenient...''

He looked at her and laughed. He had the kind of laugh that could put anyone at ease, and even though Allison was puzzled by his amusement she enjoyed it. ''No,'' he said, his eyes still sparkling as he looked at her. ''No, I can't think of a better time.''

''Well then.'' She lifted her briefcase to her lap. ''If you'll just tell me what you had in mind...''

''Nothing personal,'' he said quickly, and forcefully enough to make Allison look up at him, startled. ''That's the first thing we have to get straight.''

He was staring at her briefcase with a kind of dread fascination, as though he couldn't imagine what would be revealed when she opened it and could hardly wait to find out. *Figures,* Allison thought, and let her hands fall still on the clasp. *With a name like Stone he had to be a little strange.*

And then he looked up at her and added quickly, ''Not that you're not...I mean, not that I wouldn't like to...''

He gestured toward her in what Allison supposed was a complimentary way, and she managed a smile, albeit weak. She thought, *Not just strange, definitely case-file material.* She should have known. Had she ever been on one of these interviews in her life that hadn't turned into a disaster? If she were smart she'd pack it in now before this job ended up costing *her* money.

But then Stone smiled, and rubbed his knuckle against his chin in a rueful gesture that was irresistibly endearing, and he said, "Look, I know you're used to it, but this is really weird for me."

"I can relate to that," Allison said carefully. She was already positioning her briefcase to rise.

"You probably think I'm a real idiot. Maybe we could—I don't know—just relax and start over."

Allison hesitated, but only for a minute. Then she smiled. "I don't think you're an idiot."

"Good."

Allison decided he had a smile that could turn polar ice caps to steam. He walked over to the desk—a wide slab of obsidian glass mounted on a curved chrome base—and Allison thought he was going to sit behind it, putting professional distance between them and establishing dominance as most clients felt compelled to do sooner or later. Instead he rested one hip on the corner of the desk, folded his arms across his chest and looked as though he were inviting her to initiate a nice cozy chat. Allison found that more intimidating than if there had been a mile of desk between them.

She tried to remember Penny's advice, but it was hopeless. She just wasn't cut out to deal with the clients.

She cleared her throat and started, once again, to blunder into her sales pitch, then he said, "I'm staring. I know, and I hope you don't mind. It's just that you're not what I would have expected. I guess you hear that a lot. I like it," he added, as though to reassure her. "A real professional image, but not cold. I mean, you're cute. Is it okay if I tell you that?"

"Actually," she replied, "I hate being called cute." But her heart was beating fast with surprise and pleasure. She couldn't say she entirely objected to the turn the conversation had taken.

He grinned. "Yeah, I guess you would. I hate it when people say I look twenty-five, too, though they mean it as a compliment. I worked a long time to get *over* being twenty-five."

"Exactly," Allison agreed. "Puppies are cute, and twenty-five-year-olds are generally ignored."

"Exactly."

They shared a moment of warmth and understanding that was pure and fragile and as surprising as a burst of sunshine on a foggy day. Allison thought, *I knew I'd like him.* And she was suddenly very, very glad she had come.

Stone was amazed at how easy this was turning out to be. She could have very easily been coarse, brash and badly dressed. Not only was she attractive and quite presentable, but Stone could actually talk to her. He had a feeling he might even like her and it was hard to remember, even now, that she was only doing her job. And it was a job she did perfectly. Everything about her was perfect, and Carla was right—where else was he going to get a date for the wedding on such short notice? If you want a job well done, hire a professional. He should have thought of it himself.

He said easily, "You know, I wasn't sure this was going to work at first. But now I think it's going to be just fine."

Allison smiled, folding her hands on her briefcase. "Well, I'm certainly glad to hear that."

"So..." He glanced at her card. "Allison. Here's the situation. First things first. I have to go to my ex-wife's wedding tomorrow night—it's formal—and my ex-girlfriend left me high and dry at the last minute and I really need a date."

At her blank stare he went on quickly, "That's all it would be—just a date for the wedding, nothing more. Four or five hours, max."

Allison had certainly heard more graceful invitations in her life, but she was so surprised—and delighted—that it didn't occur to her to object. She tried to hide her amusement as she said, "You're asking me to be your date for the wedding?"

He looked momentarily uncertain. "Would that be okay? I mean, that is something you could do, right?"

Allison couldn't help it. She laughed softly. *Strange,* she thought. *But definitely worth overlooking a few eccentricities for.* "Yes," she said. "I suppose that's something I could do. Although it really is short notice." But she was thinking about the peach dress she had bought on sale at Saks last spring that she never had the chance to wear. It would be perfect for a wedding.

"So my secretary told me. But it's going to be a great wedding—lots of good food, champagne, a live band, and..." he added with another one of those heart-stopping grins, "I'm not a half-bad dancer. You might even have fun."

Allison leaned back in the chair, enjoying everything about him. "I wouldn't be a bit surprised," she murmured.

"I guess we should talk about money," he went on, "because if this works out there are some other jobs I might need you for..."

Allison laughed a little, confused. "Wait a minute, I'm not sure I—"

"So do you charge by the hour or what?"

Allison blinked. "Well, generally we charge by the job, though there are certain set fees..."

He nodded. "Of course."

"But since we really haven't talked about what you want..."

He looked a little uncomfortable. "I told you, nothing personal. Not that I don't think you're attractive—I do—and not that I wouldn't like to—well, of course I would—but let's just keep it business for now, okay? Just the wedding. How much?"

A dull ache of recognition was pushing at the back of Allison's mind and she absolutely refused to acknowledge it. She said carefully, "For what?"

"The wedding."

"What about the wedding?"

Now he looked impatient. "How much will you charge for going to the wedding with me?"

The ache turned into a burning, the suspicion into a certainty and it spread its slow, deliberate tendrils of humiliation through every nerve ending in her body. Still, almost as though to further torture herself, Allison felt compelled to repeat, in a totally expressionless voice, "You want to pay me for being your date at the wedding?"

"Well, I wouldn't expect you to do it for free. That wouldn't be right."

And then there was no way to deny it. She had set herself up for this one; she had walked right into it. She had opened her arms and *invited* humiliation... This had to be, without a doubt, the grandmother of all her disastrous interviews. Someday she would laugh about it she was sure, but right now she only wanted to get out of here.

And she had actually believed he wanted to go out with her!

She got a firm grip on her briefcase and stood stiffly, her chin held high as she turned toward the door. "Thank you for your offer, Mr. Harrison," she said in a voice Penny, with her finishing-school background, would have been proud of, "but I find I can't accept after all. Perhaps you should consider calling an escort service."

She opened the door with a single jerk and closed it firmly behind her.

Stone stood staring after her, stunned. He looked at the card in his hand, and then at the door by which she had exited. He called after her, "I thought I had!"

But of course she didn't hear.

Two

"**I**'ve always said it was a stupid name," Allison fumed. "*Party Girls!* I've always said it was stupid, always! Haven't I always said that?"

For the first two hours of her tirade, Penny had been sympathetic, even though she struggled to hide her amusement. During the second hour her reassurances had become a little absent. Now she ignored Allison entirely. But Allison didn't let her partner's lack of interest stop her. Every time her mind glanced back on the morning's mortification, her agitation returned with a surge as fresh and sharp as it had been the moment she walked out of Stone Harrison's office.

"He thought I was a . . ." But she couldn't think of a term that she hadn't used at least twice in the past three hours, and that only frustrated her further. "You *know* what he thought I was."

The telephone rang, and Penny answered it. "Party Girls." A pause, and Allison could tell by the way Penny looked at her who was on the other end. Penny covered the mouthpiece with her hand and said, "It's him again."

Allison folded her arms and turned her back.

Penny said, "Mr. Harrison I'm terribly sorry..."

The first time he had called, Allison had hung up on him. The second time his secretary had called and explained the whole gruesome mess. Allison would have felt sorry for the woman except that something about her speech sounded a little too rehearsed, and Allison could practically picture Stone Harrison standing over his secretary's shoulder scribbling out the lines that she read into the receiver. Still, he was going to an awful lot of trouble to apologize for a misunderstanding that was not his fault and only an ogre would have continued to hold a grudge. Allison was ready to forget the whole ugly scene, but within moments after his secretary had said goodbye Stone Harrison himself called and asked what time he should pick her up tomorrow evening. Allison was dumbfounded. He was amused.

She had hung up on him again. Now two bouquets of roses flanked her desk, one yellow and one red. He had called eight times in the past hour and Allison had a feeling this was turning into a battle of wills.

She should have been flattered. She was, in a secret and somewhat reluctant way, intrigued. She was also very suspicious and more than a little wary and far too embarrassed, at this point, to back down.

And that, of course, was the essence of it—she was embarrassed. She could hardly blame Stone for a mistake that, while she wouldn't go so far as to say was entirely natural, wasn't really his fault. He had certainly not intended to insult her and he had more than adequately apologized. All right, so she could blame him for not having the good taste—or good sense—to let the matter drop and disappear quietly back into the anonymity from whence he had come, but that stubborn persistence was only part of his charm—or craziness—depending on how one chose to look at it. But the truth of the matter was she was more upset with herself than with him. Even though a strong part of her wished he would just go away another even stronger part of her hoped he would not.

Penny hung up the phone with a thoughtful, speculative look on her face. "Well, that's got to be a first." She leaned back in her chair, tapping one slender, perfectly manicured finger against her chin as she regarded Allison. "We actually get a job because of one of your interviews, not in spite of it. The gentleman must be smitten."

"If that's supposed to be cute..." Allison glared at her for a moment, but Penny showed no sign of facetiousness. Curiosity warred with her better judgment and finally lost as Allison demanded, "What job? What are you talking about?"

"Frankly I don't know what he sees in you but to each his own, I suppose."

There was no mistaking the gathering storm clouds in Allison's eyes and Penny abandoned the teasing with a grin and a shrug. "A real one, as it turns out. It seems he has to give a dinner party next month for some important clients and that was what his secretary called us about in the first place."

Allison hid her relief with a disgruntled lift of her shoulders. To have blundered into the kind of social gaffe she had subjected herself to was bad enough, but to be humiliated *and* lose a job—through no fault of her own—would have been too much for one day. That something good might come of it, however small, made her feel a little better. "One dinner party," she muttered. "Big deal."

"Actually more than one. He has a whole week's worth of entertaining to do—very discreet, small scale, tasteful, exactly the kind of thing you like to do." Penny's voice was casual and Allison deliberately refrained from showing any interest. "And it's a good thing you *do* like to do it because it bores me silly, and because we only get the job if you're in charge."

Allison had known it was coming and she glared at her partner, waiting for the other shoe to drop. Penny obliged her.

"And if you'll go out with him tomorrow."

Allison turned on her heel and stalked toward the window, muffling a throaty cry of outrage and frustration. "Why is he *doing* this to me?" she demanded. "Why me?"

Penny shrugged. "Why don't you ask him yourself? Better yet, why don't you just go out with him and get it over with? What's the big deal?"

Allison rounded on her. "Are you *crazy?*"

Penny's expression became mitigated with sympathy. "That bad, huh?"

"Well, no," Allison admitted uncomfortably, "not if you're talking about looks..."

"A real jerk, though, right?"

"Well no, not exactly. In fact, he seemed really nice as far as that goes—"

"Of course!" Penny threw up her hands in a gesture of sudden enlightenment. "I get it now. He's good-looking *and* nice so naturally you can't go out with him. How could I be so silly?''

Allison turned her back on her partner with an air of sublime indifference and opened a file cabinet drawer, pretending to look for something.

''For heaven's sake, Allison, you do better in one afternoon than I've done all year and you want to throw him *back?* That's un-American!''

Allison closed the file drawer, hard. ''Come on, Penny, this is serious.''

''You bet it is. I didn't tell you what Harry said.''

And Allison didn't want to hear it. She didn't need the details, anyway. She knew the essence of it already. ''This is also,'' she said firmly, ''not an auction, and I'm *not* up for the highest bidder. Why don't you go out with him?''

''Because he didn't ask me.''

''Well, I'm sure he would if he knew you were available. He doesn't seem all that particular to me.''

''Thanks a lot.''

''Come on, Penny, he's enjoying this. Can't you see that? He embarrassed me within an inch of my life and now he just wants to rub it in.''

''For heaven's sake, *why?*''

''Because he's weird, that's why, like all our clients.''

''Well, if you ask me you're the weird one. It's a wedding, for heaven's sake. What could be more respectable than that?''

''His ex-*wife's* wedding,'' Allison corrected. ''What kind of man goes to his ex-wife's wedding...and goes to this much trouble trying to get a date?''

''The kind of man,'' suggested Penny, obviously planning the moment for its fullest impact, ''who's willing to pay us twice our going rate for one dinner party and five more nights miscellaneous entertainment—plus a fifty-percent bonus on signing?''

Allison stared at her partner. Her throat felt a little dry. ''He said that?''

Penny nodded.

''That could mean . . .''

''Enough to pay our quarterly taxes.''

Allison thought about that. She thought, as she did at least once a day every day, about getting into another line of work. She wondered exactly where one drew the line between pride and practicality and she thought a lot about Stone Harrison's smoky-gray eyes. Could anyone who looked that good be entirely bad?

''My ivory shoes would look great with your peach dress,'' Penny said thoughtfully.

Allison looked at her sharply. ''The satin shoes with the pearls?''

Penny nodded. ''And the pearl hair ornament that matches. I've only worn it once.''

Neither one of them were invited very often to the kinds of places where pearl hair ornaments and satin shoes—not to mention the peach dress—would be appropriate. And who knew how long it would be before Allison had another opportunity to attend a ritzy evening wedding? Not before the dress went out of style, that much seemed certain.

''It's probably a nudist wedding,'' she muttered. ''He's weird, his wife is probably weird, too. . .''

''Ex-wife,'' Penny reminded her. She was dialing the telephone. ''Allison Carter for Mr. Harrison, please,'' she said.

And as Allison stared at her, dumbfounded, Penny held out the receiver to her. ''Why don't you ask him if it's nudist? And even if it is, the offer of the shoes still stands," she added generously.

Allison stared at the telephone. And then, with every intention of giving Stone Harrison a piece of her mind and demonstrating to Penny exactly what strength of character was, she snatched the instrument out of Penny's hand. But she had no sooner brought the receiver to her ear than she heard Stone Harrison's voice and her resolve seemed to waver, and stick in her throat.

"Allison," he said. The warmth in his voice traveled over the wires that separated them and tingled Allison's skin...or perhaps it was simple relief she heard. "I'm glad you called. Does this mean you forgive me?"

She wanted to say, "Yes, of course." Every instinct she possessed as both a woman and a businessperson demanded that she do so. Her common sense insisted that this was the only way to get rid of him and have closure to the entire unfortunate situation. But the treacherous part of herself that didn't want to be rid of him must have been stronger than she thought because she heard herself blurting, "Why are you *doing* this to me?"

His silence seemed a little surprised. "Doing what?"

"The flowers, the phone calls..."

"Oh, that." His tone was dismissive and in the background she heard the rustle of papers. "My secretary made me do it."

"That figures."

"She says I'm selfish, demanding and insensitive."

There was more rustling in the background. The busy executive in jeans and black sweatshirt purposefully attending to business while absently tossing out charm to smooth her ruffled feathers. Allison wanted to be irritated with that. She knew she should be offended at the very least, but his technique was oddly effective—perhaps because it was so precisely off-the-cuff.

Still, she managed a scowl. "I can believe that."

"In my own defense, however, I'd like to point out that it was the first dozen roses that was my secretary's idea. The second was mine."

"Operating on the theory that if one dozen is good," she began dryly.

"Two is better. Exactly."

"Two is tacky," Allison pointed out with some satisfaction. "Two is ostentatious. You should have listened to your secretary and quit while you were ahead."

There was another small, startled pause. Then, "Oh." Allison could almost see him shrug. "I never get things like that right. I guess that's why I need somebody like you." And with a haste that was almost comical he added, "Your company, that is. My secretary told me what you really do—plan parties and business dinners and country club socials and cotillions and whatnot and I think that's fine—although the truth is, things were a lot simpler when I thought you were into another kind of social planning altogether. This whole thing is her fault, by the way, not mine."

"No one likes a man who blames someone else for his mistakes."

"True enough, but I really don't care much whether you like me. I just want you to go out with me."

Allison drew a deep, calming breath. "Mr. Harrison," she said, as pleasantly as she possibly could, "if you understand what it is we really do here then you must also know that personal favors for our clients are not among our services."

"I guess you'd be insulted if I told you that it might not be a bad idea if you did—"

"Yes." She cut him off. "I would."

"Then what can I do to persuade you to forget our bad start and be my date for tomorrow night?"

Until that moment Allison was quite prepared to respond, with perfect confidence and no regrets whatsoever, "Not a thing in this world, thank you very much." But she opened her mouth and the words wouldn't come.

Perhaps it had to do with the way he said that, with a simple, cards-on-the-table frankness that reminded her more of a man trying to negotiate a contract than of one trying to smooth-talk a woman. As a woman who had had more than her share of smooth-talking men, Allison liked that.

Perhaps it was Penny, who had been listening to Allison's side of the conversation with great interest, who chose that moment to say, "Did I mention the beaded purse that goes with the shoes?" Allison was only human, after all, and she couldn't deny the temptation. It had been *so* long since she had dressed up and gone somewhere really nice. With a not-half-bad dancer...

She exclaimed, "I don't even know you!"

"Perfect. You can't possibly have anything against me."

Penny's bright, questioning gaze was beginning to get on Allison's nerves. She turned away, sheltering the phone with one shoulder to give herself the illusion of privacy. "Listen," she said reasonably, "you can't expect me to believe that a man like you doesn't have a little black book just filled with the names of women who'd love to go out with you.''

"True," he admitted, "I do, and normally they would. But there seems to be some kind of rule about giving a woman more than twenty-four-hours notice before a formal wedding. Somebody really should write these things down."

He sounded so genuinely disgruntled that Allison had to smother a grin. "Maybe that'll be my next project. In the meantime, though..."

"Wait, don't. I know the beginning of a polite brush-off when I hear it—I should, I've heard it enough times today. Listen, you were perfectly willing to go out with me before you found out I thought you were in the business. I've apologized, you've accepted. I've sent you an ostentatious number of flowers and you've agreed to forget our previous misunderstanding, so what I want to know now is what's the problem? What's changed since you agreed to go out with me three hours ago?''

When he put it that way Allison found she had no ready answer. Penny was rummaging in the drawer behind her, and when Allison looked around Penny triumphantly held up a bottle of nail polish: peach, the same shade as her dress.

Allison frowned distractedly. "You really are very stubborn, aren't you?''

"One of my nobler qualities," he agreed.

She struggled for her resolve again and caught it by its barest edge. "The point is," she insisted, "I'm not 'in the business' as you so quaintly put it.''

"So where do you usually get dates? You meet them at work, right? You met me at work. I asked you out. You said yes. What's wrong with that?"

Perfectly reasonable. Seductively convincing.

"Think of it as a working date."

She said in exasperation, "Now that's exactly the kind of thing I'm talking about! It's not part of our service to—"

"Don't you sometimes take clients to dinner?"

"Well, of course, but—"

"So do I. Only in this case I'm taking you to a wedding. And we do still have business to discuss."

She tried to think of an argument for that, and realized that at this point she was arguing for the sake of argument...just as she strongly suspected, he was doing with her. She smiled ruefully. "You're going to an awful lot of trouble just to prove a point."

"What point?"

"That you can eventually get what you want, no matter what it takes."

There was a silence, and Allison thought she had gone too far. She was almost sorry...but not quite.

And then he chuckled softly. "I knew I was going to like you," he said. "Pick you up at six-thirty?"

"Six-thirty," Allison said, and the next thing she knew she was giving him the address.

"By the way," he said, just before he hung up, "I told you it was formal, didn't I?"

"That's right."

"Do you happen to know what that means I'm supposed to wear?"

Allison smiled. "That generally," she told him easily, "means dinner jackets for the men."

His silence suggested that was not what he had wanted to hear. Then he muttered, "Great. Now I've got to see if I have one."

She heard a click and realized he had disconnected. She stared at the dead receiver in her hand for a moment, then murmured, "If he can't find one, I wonder if the date is off?"

Then she returned the receiver to its cradle and looked at Penny, forcing a brave, if somewhat bemused smile. "Well," she said, "break out the shoes. It looks like I'm going to a wedding."

Three

___

Allison knew, of course, that she had been thoroughly manipulated. It wasn't the first time and she doubted it would be the last. But never had she been handled so deftly nor enjoyed it so thoroughly. Even though there were moments during the next day— quite a few of them—when she would stop and think, "What have I *done?*" She couldn't entirely regret having said yes.

"I still think this is a rotten way to do business," she muttered, presenting her back to Penny, who began to do up the thirty-plus tiny covered buttons that closed the back of the peach dress.

"Why does it have to be business? Why can't it just be a date?"

"Well then let me ask you this." Allison struggled with the loops that closed the twelve buttons on her lace cuffs. "Why are you so interested in making sure I go out with him?"

"Because it's good for business, of course."

"I rest my case."

Penny tugged yet another button into its tiny cloth loop. "Well, it's probably all for the best. If I ever get all these buttons fastened you're in this dress to stay, so keep it on a business level, okay?"

Allison grinned and turned her attention to the other cuff. "Somehow I don't think that'll be a problem."

"I thought you said he was gorgeous."

"I didn't say gorgeous...even though he is," she admitted. "But anyone who would try to *hire* a woman to go out with him, well, let's just say that kind of charm is usually pretty easy to resist."

"Hmm, I see what you mean." Penny finished the last button and, grasping Allison's shoulders, turned her toward the mirror. "Speaking of gorgeous..."

Allison drew in a long breath of genuine appreciation. The dress was in a style reminiscent of the twenties but with all the romance associated with the gay nineties. The peach fabric was covered with ivory lace that formed a high collar and long tight cuffs. From a dropped waist the skirt dipped in back below her calves and was gathered in front to a point even with her knees. She wore ivory stockings and Penny's elegant, pearl-trimmed ivory shoes. She had spent far too much time with a curling iron on her hair but the results were worth it—her hair was drawn away from her face in a riot of gentle curls and fastened in back by a clasp that dangled three rows of pearls. The peach shade of the dress made her skin look translucent. The gloss of a similar color on her lips widened and brightened her eyes so that they looked almost indigo. There were very few times in Allison's life when she actually felt beautiful. Today was one of them.

She smiled and nodded in satisfaction. "Okay," she agreed. "It was worth it."

They both turned toward the window at the sound of a car pulling up to the curb. "He's early," Allison said, surprised.

"Wait, don't forget these." Penny scooped up the beaded purse and lightweight evening shawl from the bed. "Got your keys?"

"Keys," Allison confirmed, "and cab fare."

"Allison, for heaven's sake!"

"Who knows? The man might be a secret drunk. My mother always said—"

"Never leave the house without cab fare home," Penny finished with a little groan. "I know, I know. My mother always said, expect the best—"

"But be prepared for the worst, I know." Allison closed the purse with a snap. The doorbell chimed downstairs and her heart beat a little faster, the way it always did when she was about to go out on a first date.

She gave her reflection one last check in the mirror, twirled a wispy curl close to her face and hurried toward the stairs. "Come on, you have to meet him."

"Looking like this?" Penny gestured to her faded jeans and chambray shirt, appalled. "Not on your life. I'll just peek through the banister at him."

Allison tossed her friend an exasperated look over her shoulder. Penny looked better in jeans and no makeup than most women—Allison included—after three hours at the beauty parlor, but tonight Allison felt too good to even resent it. The doorbell rang again and Penny gave her a little shove. "Hurry! Do you want him to give up and go away?"

Allison laughed as she hurried toward the door. Penny, true to her word, stayed at the top of the stairs, hidden behind the banister.

Allison was flushed and a little breathless as she opened the door. What she saw took her breath completely away. There, in the soft yellow glow of her porch light stood, what was without a doubt, the best-looking man she had ever seen outside a movie theater. He wore a white dinner jacket with a negligent ease James Bond might have envied. The last time she had seen him his hair had been tumbled down over his forehead in vagrant waves and curls, battered by impatient fingers. Now it was brushed smoothly away from his face, yet the way it curled over his collar in back, just an inch or two too long, gave him a rakish look. When he looked at her his eyes took on a smoldering glint that made her heart beat even faster.

She wanted to say, "Wow!" and caught herself just in time. She said instead, "I see you found a dinner jacket."

"I see you found...everything." His eyes moved over her, from the freshly curled hair to the lace-covered shoulders to the barest hint of cleavage before the peach underdress began, then down across her abdomen and to the ruffle at her knees and the tips of her ivory-colored, pearl-trimmed slippers. Simple, unadorned sincerity rang in his voice as he said, "You look great...you really do." Then, looking rather pleased with himself, he added, "This is going to work out fine."

Allison had a feeling she probably should have been insulted by that last remark—reminiscent of the way a man might comment on a new car or a suite of rooms—but she didn't want to spoil the moment. Besides, it was hard to be insulted by anything when he was looking at her that way. So she smiled, and stepped away from the door, gesturing. "Would you like to come in?"

She could practically feel Penny straining for a glimpse through the doorway.

He looked over her shoulder into the room beyond, and there was a hint of regret in his voice as he answered, "I guess not. Seems I made a mistake about the time, it starts at seven, not seven-thirty so we'd better go." He turned toward the street, gesturing toward a long, gray limousine gleaming in the reflected light of her doorway. "The bar's stocked, so we can have a drink on the way."

Then Allison couldn't resist. "Wow," she said softly. She turned quickly and pulled the door closed. Penny would just have to fend for herself. "Nice car."

He grinned and touched her arm lightly as they went down the steps. "The one thing no one ever accused me of was a lack of class."

"I'll say. Is it yours?"

"Just hired for the evening. I figured there might be parking problems. Also, I wanted to impress you."

Allison glanced up at him, amused. "Consider me impressed."

"Perfect. I love having money. It makes everything so much easier."

"I wouldn't know," Allison murmured as the chauffeur opened the door for her. She climbed inside the plush gray-and-mahogany interior and decided that if this was what having money was about she could get used to it very easily. There was a small television in the corner nearest her; the screen was blank but the overhead stereo speakers softly piped in the lilting strains of Vivaldi. The compact bar opposite her was stocked with dozens of tiny bottles of liquor, fresh juices and mixers and half-bottles of wine. There was a covered ice bucket next to it in which Allison imagined a bottle of champagne cooled, but just before Stone settled beside her she peeked inside and found it contained nothing but ice.

"So," Stone invited, examining the labels on the small liquor bottles. "What would you like?"

Allison hesitated. "Nothing, I suppose. I'd only spill it on my dress."

Stone grinned. "I don't know, the Rolls people make a pretty smooth-riding car. And Jeff's a good driver, aren't you, Jeff?"

The driver glanced in the rearview mirror. "I try, sir."

"How about a martini," he suggested. "It's clear, and if you spill it, no one will notice. Do you know how to mix a martini?"

He was busily picking up and putting down bottles, presumably looking for the gin, and Allison quickly lifted her hand in a gesture of capitulation. "All right, club soda. That won't stain. With ice."

"White wine," Stone decided. "That way we can both have a glass." He selected a bottle. "Do you know anything about wine?"

"I know everything about wine. It's my job. But I'd rather have club soda."

Stone applied the corkscrew to the small bottle. "I hope you're not too particular. I'd be willing to bet this is not one of your snob-appeal vintages."

She stared at him as he poured two glasses of wine. "You're a real take-charge kind of guy, aren't you?"

"Most people would say 'selfish and inconsiderate.'"

"Who am I to argue with most people?"

But he gave her another one of those heart-stopping grins as he handed her a glass of wine. "Come on," he persuaded, "I want to make a toast."

Under those circumstances she couldn't refuse, and she was glad she had not when in the next moment he lifted his glass to her. "To Allison," he said. "Who saved my life."

Allison smiled and gave a rueful shake of her head. "You're impossible. Do people tell you that, too?"

"All the time." He took a sip of his wine. "But I'm serious. I can't tell you how much I appreciate this."

Allison gestured cavalierly, a little embarrassed by his sincerity. "Hey, for a free limo ride and all the white wine I can drink..."

"It's just that Melinda, that's my ex-wife, is kind of—how shall I put this?—overprotective. She worries about me all of the time. And if I showed up at her wedding without a date I'd never hear the end of it."

Allison glanced down at her wineglass, forming the question carefully. "I know this is none of my business, but I can't help wondering...I mean, it just seems a little strange to me, that you'd go to this much trouble just to be able to attend your ex-wife's wedding."

He lifted one shoulder negligently, leaning back against the seat. "I guess so. But my whole family is a little strange."

Allison tried not to look too curious, but he smiled and explained, "Melinda's not your typical ex-wife.

We grew up together, got married more because people expected us to than because we wanted to. It took about eight months for us to realize we'd made a mistake—or for Melinda to realize it. Fortunately, or sometimes unfortunately, I think, marriage didn't ruin our friendship. She worries that she broke my heart." He took another sip of wine. "I sometimes worry because she didn't."

There was a hidden meaning behind that statement and Allison found herself intensely interested in exploring it. But as Penny often pointed out, one of Allison's most annoying characteristics was her tendency to want to organize people in the same way she organized her business, and she had to stop the probing questions and the instinctive insights that leapt to her tongue with an effort. Stone Harrison's personal life was none of her business. All that was required of her tonight—and in fact for the rest of their relationship—was that she make polite conversation and try not to offend him.

So she said, "How long have you been divorced?"

"Almost five years. And believe me, no one is as happy about the wedding as I am. Being married will give Melinda something to do."

"And you're sure she won't mind your coming with a date?"

Stone laughed softly. "Are you kidding? She'll be thrilled. Particularly with you." His eyes moved over her once more, assessively, and he nodded approvingly. "You're exactly the type of girl she would have picked out for me. Wholesome, refined. Nice."

With an effort, Allison swallowed back a wave of indignation. "You make me sound like a loaf of bread."

He chuckled and lifted his glass to her again. "But only the highest quality bread. You know," he added, taking another sip of wine. "After you left yesterday, I took your advice and called an escort service. Even *they* couldn't fix me up with anybody on such short notice—not anyone suitable for a wedding, anyway. So you really did save my life, Allison, and I can't tell you how much I appreciate it."

Allison was glad she didn't like white wine. She no doubt would have choked at that point. Indignation blossomed into outrage and for a long time all she could do was stare at him. Stone, his perfectly regular features arranged into a portrait of contentment, gazed out the window at the passing lights, completely oblivious.

When Allison's voice returned it was all she could do to keep it even. She managed, very calmly, "Let me get this straight. I was second choice to a *hooker?*"

He looked back at her. "Call girl," he corrected. "And it wasn't even a contest. You were always my first choice."

Allison took a deep breath. "And that's why the flowers, the phone calls—because the escort service turned you down?"

He nodded, completely unabashed. "Of course by that time I was pretty desperate, and I don't mind saying you gave me a few bad moments. But the important thing is that you came around in the end, and like I said, I can't thank you enough."

The car made a turn and glided to a stop. Allison set her wineglass in the recessed holder on the bar, mostly to prevent herself from flinging the contents into his face. He smiled at her and said, "Here we are."

Allison managed a stiff smile. *Be polite.* The voice inside her head sounded like Penny's. *He's a client.* And so she said, very politely, "Do people ever tell you you're also a jerk?"

He displayed only the mildest surprise. "Sometimes. Apparently not often enough. I said something to insult you, right?"

Allison's outrage turned into a kind of disbelieving dismay. How could anyone be so thoroughly objectionable and at the same time so impossible to reprimand? How *did* he get away with it? And why did she find it so impossible to stay angry with him?

The chauffeur opened the door for her, and she dragged her gaze away from Stone with difficulty. She cleared her throat but couldn't entirely keep the brittleness out of her voice as she replied, "Insult me? Don't be silly."

She turned to leave the car but Stone touched her arm. His expression was serious, the set of his lips self-recriminatory. "I did insult you," he said. "Of course I did. I'm an idiot sometimes. Don't ask me why, I just am—the way some people are always late or have bad haircuts. I'm sorry. Believe me, the last person in the world I want to offend right now is you."

There was absolutely no denying the sincerity of his tone, and when his expression gentled, coaxing a smile from her, she knew exactly how he got away with it.

"I'll tell you what," he offered, "if you promise not to hold it against me, you can have free license to tell me whenever I'm behaving like a jerk and I won't hold it against you. How does that sound?"

His eyes were warm in the dim courtesy light of the car, his smile as alluring as a caress, his tone inviting confidence and trust. Allison hesitated, but she was beginning to discover what she suspected dozens of women had learned before her—Stone Harrison was very nearly impossible to resist. She tried, unsuccessfully, to smother a smile. "It sounds like you have got a deal," she replied.

He relaxed, smiling broadly. "I promise you won't regret it."

Allison's own smile deepened into ruefulness as she got out of the car and she murmured, mostly to herself, "You'd better believe it."

Not even Stone—thoughtless, incorrigible, guilelessly arrogant as he was—could interfere with Allison's enjoyment of the wedding. Allison loved weddings. She didn't care what kind of wedding, where it was, whose it was, whether it was formal or casual, indoors or out, whether the ceremony was religious or secular. She more than loved weddings—she adored them, reveled in them.

She was completely swept away by the pageantry and spectacle. The symbolism behind the ritual enchanted her: the groomsmen, tall and stalwart, who in days of yore would have worn swords and formed a living shield around the groom as they escorted him to the place of meeting with his bride, protecting him from his enemies or the bride's irate kinsmen; the maids and matrons of honor who would once have represented the bride's dowry and whose duty it would have been to not only attend her every comfort, but to protect her virtue until she was delivered into the hands of her final protector, her husband. It was all so ancient and thrilling, one of civilization's rare remaining links into its dim and murky past. When it was done right the ceremony, from beginning to end, brought a chill of wonder to Allison's skin.

Melinda knew how to do it right. The church was a fairyland of salmon roses and ivory candles. Banks of roses—all in that precise salmon hue—greeted guests in the vestibule, shimmering in the muted light of a dozen swaying candle flames, roses climbed the walls and formed two arches between the aisles, sprays of roses trimmed with ivory satin ribbon decorated each pew. A pink satin runner lined the aisle and ended at the rose-trimmed arbor flanked by two elaborate candelabra at the front of the church. The overhead lighting was dimmed to such an extent that the illusion was that the entire church was lit by the flickering glow of strategically placed candelabra. The entire effect was elegant but not ostentatious, romantic but not sappy.

She and Stone were almost late. A tenor and a soprano were finishing up the last strains of a heart-rending duet, and as soon as Allison and Stone were seated, two boys in cutaways began rolling up the salmon-colored runner while two more, directly behind them, unfurled an ivory one. Stone looked around appreciatively. "Well," he murmured, "it looks like she's marrying money. Good for her."

Allison said, "Shh," as the prelude to the Wedding March began. The procession was led by a little girl in a frilly lace dress randomly flinging rose petals from her basket, and Allison settled back in utter bliss to enjoy the ceremony.

From the moment she had decided to attend the wedding she had been unabashedly curious to find out exactly what the ex-wife of a man such as Stone Harrison would look like. She had noticed that successful

men, particularly good-looking successful men, had
a tendency to pick their wives and lovers according to
dress size more often than not, which proved nothing
except they were men. Allison had a picture formed in
her head of the ex-Mrs. Harrison: blond, full busted,
slim hipped, generically beautiful and exquisitely
groomed, an ex-model or near model. Not that there
was anything wrong with that—the description she
had provided for herself of Melinda Harrison could
also fit her best friend Penny. It was just that Allison
was surprised to find the other woman was nothing as
she had imagined.

First of all she was dark haired, and even on this
formal occasion she wore her hair dressed simply,
pulled back from her face and pinned into a double
knot from which a cascade of gauze veil fluttered to
her waist. She had an open, friendly face—which of
course looked radiant on this occasion—and a nice
figure that was by no means fashion-model material.
Allison liked her on sight, which puzzled her because
she couldn't figure out why Stone had liked her. But
then again, he had divorced her.

The bride wore a salmon-colored gown and her at-
tendants wore ivory, which Allison thought was a delightful twist on the usual theme and a perfect choice
for a second wedding. The ceremony was interspersed
with poetry readings and musical selections. Melinda
married a distinguished-looking man with gray at his
temples who obviously adored her, and when the
wedding couple was introduced and made their tri-
umphant recession to the celebratory chords of
Lohengrin, Allison noticed that her eyes were wonderfully, sentimentally misty.

She discreetly dabbed at the corner of her eyes as the music died down and the crowd began to shuffle into the aisles. "It was a lovely ceremony," she said earnestly to Stone. "Thank you for inviting me."

He glanced at his watch. "It was a little long, if you ask me. When we got married it took four minutes, I timed it. If I had known this was going to take so long I would have eaten dinner first. I'm starved."

Allison stared at him, standing still even though she was blocking the aisle. "You *timed* your wedding?"

He touched her arm to gesture her out of the way, smiling at someone over her shoulder. "Of course it was nothing like this—just a J.P. and a courthouse one Saturday afternoon. I guess Melinda always wanted a fancy wedding. Women are silly about things like that sometimes."

"Aren't they just?" Allison said, shaking her head a little in disbelief.

He caught her look and its meaning and he insisted, "What? Now this doesn't qualify for jerkdom, it's just common sense. You're just as married whether it takes four minutes or forty and all that poetry and candlelight doesn't have a thing to do with it."

As he spoke he was edging her through the crowd, occasionally lifting his hand to an acquaintance or nodding a greeting, and Allison tried to hide her exasperation. It was, after all, a wedding and she was his date. Her job was to look pleasant. But that did not keep her from replying, "That's not the point. It's the gesture, don't you see, the symbolism, the ritual—the *memories* that are important. Those are the things a woman will carry with her for the rest of her life—and sometimes those things outlast the marriage."

"I rest my case."

"Oh, for heaven's sake." She couldn't prevent the annoyance in her tone. "Don't you know anything at all about romance?"

"I know a lot about romance," he insisted. "I sent the roses, didn't I?"

When she looked at him his eyes were twinkling and she was reminded once again just how difficult it was to stay at odds with him about anything. He said, "You're really nice, and you look great in that dress, but you don't have much of a sense of humor, do you?"

Allison smiled sweetly. "I have a great sense of humor. I went out with you, didn't I?"

He laughed, and the way his eyes crinkled at the corners and his fingers squeezed her arm, just a little, with a warm, friendly pressure, made her forget that she had not intended to amuse him. *Impossible,* Allison repeated to herself, and her amazement rose another notch. He was utterly impossible...and without a doubt the most interesting man she had been out with all year.

The reception was being held at a private club, and even though Stone made an unseemly rapid departure from the church—the buffet table, after all, was waiting—the circular driveway was packed with cars when they arrived. Lights were blazing, red-jacketed valets were scurrying back and forth, music and laughter spilled through the open doors as gaily dressed guests paraded up the walk.

Stone tapped his fingers against the armrest impatiently. "There'll probably be a reception line," he grumbled.

Allison replied, amused, "It's customary, at weddings."

"It's ridiculous. Everyone already knows them or they wouldn't be here. The trouble with weddings is the trouble with life—it takes too long to get to the good part."

And before Allison could do more than register a gurgle of astonished laughter, he caught her hand and opened the door. "You don't mind walking, do you? Those shoes don't look too uncomfortable, and it's not far."

Allison soon discovered it didn't matter whether she minded or not as she scrambled to keep up with him. He kept his hand lightly on her arm and his stride was so long as he deftly wove in and around the other guests, calling out greetings but never stopping or even slowing down, that Allison finally gasped, "Stop, for heaven's sake! I'm not going in there all sweaty and windblown."

He barely spared her a glance as he cupped her elbow and urged her up the stairs. "You look fine. If we don't hurry, the line is going to be all the way out the door. Whoever would have thought Melinda knew so many people?"

She glared at him but as she had already learned, trying to dissuade Stone from any course of action once he had made up his mind was futile at best.

The reception line began only a few feet beyond the cloakroom, and at last Stone was forced to stop, although he couldn't seem to resist shifting his position to peer in front, trying to see how many people were ahead of them. Allison could feel her ringlets sagging and hair spray melting as an entire afternoon of painstaking hair sculpting fell victim to a five-minute walk from the car. She attempted to make discreet repairs to her hairstyle but found it was almost impossible with no mirror.

She touched Stone's arm. "If you'll excuse me, I think I'll try to find a powder room and repair the damage the race did to my hair."

"Oh, no you don't." He caught her arm before she could slip away. "We're not giving up this place in line, we'll be here all night. Besides, you look fine, you look great. Just stay put, you can go in a few minutes."

"Well, of all the—!"

But she never finished her indignant exclamation, not that she probably would have done so in public anyway, because the couple in front of Stone turned to greet him. That seemed to distract him from his concerns about how long the line was, and he fell into an easy conversation with them. Allison waited for him to introduce her to his friends, each of whom would occasionally cast curious, expectant glances toward her, but Stone was oblivious. Allison smiled at them feebly and let her gaze wander away. She wanted to pinch Stone, but doubted if even that would remind him of his manners. Someday someone was going to have to teach him a lesson, and she only hoped she could be around to watch.

It didn't occur to her until the very next moment that she might be the one to actually do it.

"Well, do my eyes deceive me? Can that handsome young man be the famous Gregory Harrison?"

Allison lifted an eyebrow and murmured, "Gregory?"

The voice belonged to a middle-aged woman in a periwinkle-blue sheath and matching cape. The sheath was a little tight for her and the cape far too dramatic, but she wore them both with such an elegant flair it didn't matter. Her salt-and-pepper hair was swept up and away from her face in a modified pompadour and accented with a diamond cat pin. Her eyes swept Allison with a greedy curiosity that made her hold her shoulders a little straighter even as she at the same time fought the urge to hide behind Stone.

Stone's eyes danced as he moved to kiss the woman's cheek. "And if isn't the belle of the ball. I'm glad to see you were able to sneak away from your parole officer in time to make it."

"Hush, you terrible boy. Do you want someone to hear you?" She slapped at his arm but her eyes never left Allison. "And where are your manners, for heaven's sake? Who is this lovely creature?"

At last, Allison thought dryly.

Stone said, "Stella Blake, may I present Allison Carter, my—"

And that was when inspiration struck. A small stab for justice, a minor payback for the list of offenses that began with Stone putting her in second place behind a prostitute and ended with him ruining her hairstyle and ignoring her in front of his friends. And he said she had no sense of humor!

She stepped forward smoothly, extending her hand with a smile. "Fiancée," she supplied warmly. "What a pleasure to meet you, Ms. Blake."

But the other woman ignored Allison's hand, and she had a terrible feeling her little practical joke was sinking. Stella Blake stared at her, her lips trembling, her eyes filling with tears. And before Allison could do more than cast a frantic, apologetic look toward Stone the other woman exclaimed, "Oh . . . my dear!" And swept Allison into her arms.

Trapped and stunned, Allison found herself the center of attention from everyone around them. She tried to twist around so that she could see Stone but he was no help whatsoever.

He said, deadpan, "Allison, say hello to my mother."

Four

____

Stone knew he should rescue Allison, but at first he was too surprised, and then he was too amused. Then he looked at Allison, caught in his mother's formidable embrace and looking very much as if she were a small brown rabbit trapped by a big friendly bear and he thought, *Serves her right.*

He knew why she had done it, of course. First his remarks about the length of the ceremony then his insistence on rushing through the reception line. She thought she would break a cog in the wheel of his intentions and he couldn't entirely blame her. He very often inspired women to small acts of rebellion that came under the heading of For Your Own Good and Teaching You a Lesson. He didn't understand the reasoning behind these little demonstrations of willfulness and wasn't sure he wanted to, but he had to admit this one baffled him more than most. What could she possibly expect to prove by telling his mother she was engaged to him?

His mother exclaimed, "Gregory, you wretch, you ungrateful child, how *could* you keep such a secret! And here I was worried sick about you, starting to drag out my list of friends with unmarried daughters—which is getting a little worn, let me assure you—and all the while you're secretly engaged. How could you?"

And that was when Stone thought, *Serves them both right.*

His mother was a dear soul and he loved her immensely, but for the past five years or so she had started to obsess on the idea of his settling down to raise a family. As a matchmaker she was almost as bad as Melinda, and it had gotten to the point that he kept her as ill informed as possible about his social life. Still, she always seemed to find out when he was currently unattached and that was when his misery began. The round of introductions, the small dinner parties, the theater tickets and the "daughter of an old friend just in town for the evening," even lectures on the dangers of single life in today's permissive society.

And it wasn't just her. Everyone he knew seemed to know the perfect woman for him, and he was in for a never-ending string of blind dates and sisters of friends and friends of sisters the moment the word got out about his breakup with Susan. Of course, at a gathering this size the word would be out in a matter of minutes and he'd spend the entire evening dancing with women he didn't know and making excuses why he couldn't call them on Monday, unless...

Someone clapped him on the back, "Stone you old dog, is it true?"

And a female hand pressed his arm. "I can't believe it! Stone Harrison, the last of the holdouts!"

While his mother embraced Allison again and declared, "I can't believe he didn't tell his own mother! Well, never you mind my dear, that's only one of the things you have to learn about my son—he has absolutely *no* sense of propriety. And for that I simply refuse to take the blame."

Allison was beginning to look desperate as she tried to wriggle out of his mother's arms. "Actually, Mrs. Harrison—I mean, Blake—"

"Second marriage, my dear. He was a sweetheart but had less than ten good years left in him by the time I got him. You call me Stella."

"I, uh, thank you, Mrs.—I mean, Stella. But I'm afraid—that is—"

For a moment Stone enjoyed Allison's scarlet-faced, tongue-tied misery, but he didn't want to let it go too far. He stepped in smoothly, drew her close with an arm around her shoulders and said, "Now darling, you see what you've done? I told you this would happen if you let it slip." He addressed his mother over Allison's stunned, round-eyed gaze. "We wanted to surprise you," he said, giving Allison's shoulders an affectionate little squeeze as he glanced down at her. "But now you've gone and spoiled it, haven't you?"

His mother's eyes narrowed just a fraction as she looked at him, but then she turned back to Allison with a warm smile, "Don't pay any attention to him, dear. You and I are going to settle back and have a nice long talk."

Allison stammered, "But—"

"Stone! Stone, darling!"

It was the bride, and to his delight Stone saw she was beckoning them to the front of the line. "Excuse me, Mother," he said, and pulled Allison away.

Allison almost regained coherency before they reached the bride and groom. "Are you crazy?" she gasped. "I can't believe you let her think—"

And Stone replied innocently, "I only let her think what you told her."

"I didn't know she was your mother, for heaven's sake!"

Stone smiled. "I love a good joke, don't you?"

Allison couldn't reply, even if she had known what to say—even if she could have controlled her shock and indignation long enough to say it—because they had reached the bridal couple. She decided to make a new rule: simple, hardworking, earnest folks such as she should never give into mischievous impulses or play practical jokes; they simply couldn't get away with it. People such as Stone, on the other hand, could obviously get away with anything.

Stone kissed the bride and heartily shook the hand of the groom, who Allison thought was a doctor of some sort, very good-looking and obviously well-off. When Stone introduced her, she murmured what she hoped were appropriate congratulatory remarks while she tried to edge unobtrusively away. She should have known better.

Melinda declared, "Stone Harrison, only you would do something like this, and at my wedding for heaven's sake! What have you got to say for yourself? No, don't say anything." She turned to Allison, her eyes bright and sparkling with the joy of the day and avid curiosity. "Is it true? Stone is a horrible tease and I never believe a word he says, so tell me—are you really engaged?''

Allison opened her mouth to reply and quite adamantly, but Stone's arm clamped around her shoulders again and he said, ''Is your heart going to be broken if we are?''

Melinda tossed back her head and laughed. ''Broken? If I weren't already the happiest woman in the world...'' She slipped her arm through that of her new husband with an adoring look. ''This would do it.''

Stone said, in a tone just odd enough to make Allison look up at him curiously, ''You mean that, don't you?''

Melinda was glowing. ''Of course I do. To have you settled, and as happy as I am, of course I do. Although...'' She pretended annoyance. ''I may never forgive you for not telling me. How could you keep a secret like this from me?''

It had gone far enough and Allison opened her mouth to set the record straight but once again Stone intervened. ''This is your day,'' he said smoothly. ''We didn't want to steal your sunshine. And it's still your day, so eat your cake and open your presents and forget about us.''

She laughed again. ''Are you kidding? You've already given me the best present I could have.''

Stone leaned forward and kissed Melinda's cheek. ''Happy wedding, kiddo. And have a great life.''

Melinda smiled warmly at Allison. ''You and I are going to be great friends. As soon as I get back from my honeymoon we'll have lunch. We have so much to talk about!''

Allison stammered, ''You—you had a beautiful wedding.''

Stone dragged her away.

"That," Allison said tightly, "was the cruelest thing I've ever seen. First you lie to your mother, then to a bride on her wedding day! You're a guest in the woman's home, for heaven's sake—"

"Clubhouse," Stone replied absently. "Besides, it's rented."

"And you stand right there and *lie* to her, making a perfect fool out of her, not to mention me! She's a nice woman and she doesn't deserve to be treated like this. I'm going to clear the whole thing up right now!"

She whirled on her heel but once again Stone caught her arm in a graceful, almost choreographic movement that somehow resulted in her turning around, sitting down and ending up with a glass of champagne in her hand. "Now hold on just a minute," he said, helping himself to another glass of champagne from the tray just before the waiter carried it out of reach. "We should talk about this."

"Talk about what?" Allison insisted. "Okay, I admit it—you're better at practical jokes than I am, is that what you want to hear? But I'm not going to be a party to this a minute longer. I'm either telling the bride the truth right now or I'm leaving."

The bench onto which Stone had forced her was small, velvet and bedecked with flowers, arranged in an alcove that Allison suspected was designed for photo opportunities. It was just roomy enough for one comfortably or two very intimate people. When she tried to rise Stone blocked her way and it was easy to see there would be no escape without his cooperation.

He said, "Relax, drink your champagne. Let's just talk about this for a minute."

From her position on the bench Allison had a perfect view of lean, well-dressed masculine thighs and pelvis and not much else. She had to tilt her head back to glare at him, which irritated her. "Talk all you like, but it's going to take more than one glass of champagne to convince me to go through with this charade."

He grinned. "Good thing there's more where that came from then."

Unexpectedly he moved to sit beside her. She pressed herself into the padded arm of the bench but it seemed there wasn't one part of his body that didn't touch hers at some point—his thigh, warm and hard against hers, his knee, his hip pressing their counterparts on her body, his arm and shoulder brushing against hers. She tried to sit up straight and meet his eyes on their own level but it was difficult to do. His nearness was a little overwhelming and even moreso because he seemed completely oblivious to the physical contact or the discomfort it was causing her—the confidence of a man who was so accustomed to intimacy with women that it was second nature to him. Those smoky-gray eyes were close enough to hypnotize. Allison tried to look away and found that she couldn't.

He said earnestly, "Look, I know you've already done me one big favor by coming here..."

Allison took a long drink of champagne to steady her senses. "Don't try that sincere act with me, okay? I've fallen for it once too often already."

"I'm not being sincere," he countered. "I'm just being honest. Look, if you tell Melinda the truth now she'll be mad at me, she'll be mad at you, it'll ruin her wedding day and I'll have to go home without anything to eat.''

Allison rolled her eyes in exasperation but before she could say anything, he went on quickly, ''She's leaving on her honeymoon in a couple of hours and won't be back in town for a month. Why spoil things for her? Didn't you hear her say this was the best present anyone could give her?''

Allison hesitated. There were several things she could say about a man whose ex-wife was *that* happy to see him become someone else's problem. But there were just as many things to be said for a man who would be that concerned about the happiness of a woman he hadn't loved in five years. She wasn't sure she understood either situation and, not understanding, was reluctant to criticize.

But Melinda had seemed delighted, and was there any harm in letting her continue to think that all was right with the world on her wedding day? By the time she got home from her honeymoon Stone could tell her whatever he liked; it was certain that Allison would never see her again. Besides it seemed a great deal more awkward to tell the truth at this point than to let the lie stand.

Allison caught herself, appalled, staring at the glass in her hand. Either the champagne was a great deal more potent than she had imagined, or Stone's bedroom-soft eyes and gentle persuasions were. Could she really be considering agreeing to this insane charade?

She shook her head adamantly, more to convince herself than Stone. ''No. It's crazy. I can't pretend to be engaged to you, I don't even know you! Your own mother—''

"I'll keep her away from you, I promise. There are over five hundred people here, it won't be hard to avoid her—or Melinda, either, for that matter. All you have to do is smile a lot and look like you adore me and you were planning to do that anyway, weren't you? And of course," he added, "don't deny it when I introduce you as my fiancée."

It was his eyes, Allison decided, and took another deep drink from the champagne glass. Definitely his eyes. Warm and embracing, with just a hint of a smile far back in their depths that made a woman feel as though, when he spoke to her, he was trusting her with his most cherished secrets . . . or most secret desires.

It was with a determined effort that she shook herself free of his spell. "Mr. Harrison," she began firmly.

"Stone. My name is Stone."

She hesitated, then looked at him curiously. "May I ask you something?"

He seemed to relax a fraction as he tasted his champagne. His arm rubbed against hers when he lifted his glass but what was an accidental touching felt very much like a caress. "Anything at all."

"What does Stone stand for?"

His eyes twinkled. "I'm not sure we know each other well enough for that."

She frowned a little and lifted her own glass, trying to inch further into the corner as he lowered his arm and she felt the press of his muscles against her lace-covered shoulder again. His scent was of crisp, expensive fabric and woodland herbs—rich, intoxicating, forbidden.

She said with some difficulty, "Fair enough. And we certainly don't know each other well enough for you to ask me for a favor like this."

"Not even if I beg?"

"Oh, for pity's sake." Her tone was exasperated as she tried, once again, to get to her feet.

Once again he detained her, this time with a hand lightly upon hers. "Look," he said, "I don't know how to say this without sounding like a jerk, but do you know what it's like to be an unmarried, heterosexual male in my age and tax bracket in this city today?"

Allison eyed him skeptically. "All I know is that yesterday afternoon you were ready to pay somebody to go out with you."

He made a dismissing gesture. "That's beside the point. What I'm trying to say is that when you *are* an unmarried man like me, women come out of the woodwork, with hooks and claws—"

Allison muffled an indignant exclamation and started to surge to her feet; he held her wrist, looking impatient.

"What I mean is that every well-meaning friend and relative within a hundred miles is constantly doing their best to try to help me meet the right woman and, to tell you the truth, it gets to be a hassle. Everyone I know is in this room tonight and if they find out I'm unattached again . . ." He left the sentence unfinished as though the picture suggested was too hideous for words. "But a few painless hours of pretending on your part could save me days—maybe weeks—of misery. So what do you say?"

Allison looked at him steadily. "You are autocratic, overbearing, chauvinistic and conceited. I can't think of a reason in this world why I should be in the least bit inclined to help you out."

He let the first part of her speech completely pass over him and seized on the last. "I'll make it worth your while of course. I wouldn't expect you to—"

Allison's hand tightened on her nearly empty glass meaningfully. "If you offer to pay me..."

He grinned quickly and lifted a hand in self-defense. "Of course not. But this would really mean a lot to me, and if you'll go along with it I'd be happy to give you..."

Something about Allison's expression must have warned him because he paused. She invited coolly, "What? Just what will you give me?"

He smiled, and it was an utterly enchanting gesture. She did not have to be touching him to feel it go all the way through her, but since she was the effect was like sunshine creeping through her skin. He said, "How about a kiss?"

Her pulse started to beat a little faster and though she tried not to she couldn't keep her gaze from straying to his lips. He had a wonderful mouth, strong but not harsh, swift to humor yet sensuous. His lips would be soft, but demanding. Experimentative, bold, coaxing...

She swallowed hard and met his eyes coolly, doing her best to disguise the train of her thoughts. "You must think your kisses are pretty valuable."

"I wouldn't know," he admitted modestly. "But some people seem to think so. And if that's not enough—haven't you ever done anything just for the fun of it?"

Her eyebrows flew up. "You think acting out a lie for the benefit of over five hundred friends and relatives is *fun?*"

"Sure, why not? What have you got to lose?"

Allison looked into those deep-warm, dancing gray eyes and she thought a little dizzily, *What, indeed?*

Later of course she would want to blame it on the wine, or even devilishly seductive dancing gray eyes. But the truth was this was a woman who had once set out to hitchhike to New Orleans, who had almost run away to Europe with an artist, who had sat on her living-room floor regarding Penny over an empty bottle of wine and a stack of unpaid bills and had said, "Why not?" And it had been too long since she had done anything just for the fun of it. Just to be reckless and daring and irresponsible for a little while, to let someone else worry about the consequences. What, after all, did she have to lose?

So she looked at Stone, drained her glass and said, "Why not?"

A mixture of relief and surprise brightened his face but only for a minute. Then he was all business again. "Great," he said. He grasped her hands and pulled her to her feet. "Now that that's settled let's eat. Maybe you could pretend to faint and we could get in the front of the line."

Allison cast him a sour look. "That'd better be one hell of a kiss," she muttered.

His eyes twinkled as he dropped his hand to her waist in a gesture of absent affection. "The world will stop spinning,' he promised her.

"I can hardly wait."

Stone laughed softly and gestured her to precede him. "Oddly enough," he murmured, mostly to himself, "neither can I."

The chances were good that if Allison had known what she was really getting into she might never have agreed. The building was huge, the festivity rampant, and despite Stone's claims that everyone he knew was here, how many of the guests could actually care one way or the other whether Stone Harrison was engaged? And among those who did, how many of them could Allison possibly meet in the few hours she was going to be there?

As a matter of fact she lost count: She had thought Penny had a wide circle of acquaintances, but even her popularity paled in comparison with that of Stone Harrison. People he worked with, people he had done business with, people he had gone to school with, people who knew his mother, people who knew Melinda, people he had once dated and people whose girlfriends he had once dated—all of them stopped by with a clap on the shoulder, a kiss on the cheek, a congratulatory word or two and a long thorough look at Allison. Stone took it all in stride and did not let any of it detract from his enjoyment of the buffet. And when yet another perfect stranger squeezed her arm confidentially and declared, "Do you have any idea what a prize you've snared? How on earth did you catch him?" Allison returned a frozen smile and replied, "With a net."

Stone abandoned the salmon mousse long enough to interject, "You see, Carolyn, I told you I'd never marry anybody who didn't have a sense of humor."

Carolyn, it was easy to see, was a perfect example of that particular deficit, and it was perhaps that, or maybe it was the catty little look Carolyn cast her, that made Allison's protective instincts bristle. Or perhaps it was the fact that Carolyn simply wouldn't go away.

Carolyn sidled close to Stone and threaded her arm through his. Stone, who was trying to balance a plate in one hand and utensils in the other, did a quick little juggling act to keep from dropping both. "But this is just too mysterious," Carolyn purred. "You must tell me everything. How did you meet?"

"At work," Stone answered and tried, without much success, to unobtrusively disengage his arm.

Carolyn laughed lightly and humorously. "Now why doesn't that surprise me?"

"Actually," Allison put in blithely, "we were fighting over a parking space." The words rolled off her tongue, and her imagination did the rest. "I thought he was the rudest, most arrogant—"

Stone cast her an admiring look and embellished effortlessly, "And I thought she was on work-release from the mental hospital. She drove like a crazy person. Still does, as a matter of fact."

"To make a long story short," Allison went on happily, "our bumpers locked—"

"Now *that's* romance. And when I found out she was my eleven o'clock—"

"When I found out *he* was Stone Harrison—"

"It was love at first sight," Stone concluded, and they looked at each other fondly.

Carolyn murmured uncertainly, "How...sweet."

Allison stepped forward to help him with the plate, which was perilously close to spilling all over Carolyn's low-cut, full-skirted black-and-white gown. "Here, honey, let me take that before you make a mess." Her impulse was to give the plate a little nudge in the right direction but she controlled herself just in time, turning a saccharine smile on Carolyn. "Sometimes he's simply helpless, do you know what I mean?"

In order for Stone to relinquish the plate it was necessary for Carolyn to relinquish his arm, and she looked annoyed at that. Allison went on chattily, "Of course it's really my fault—I was late getting home and we didn't have any dinner..."

Carolyn lifted an eyebrow. "Are you living together then? But I thought—"

Allison tried to look chagrined as she turned to Stone. "Oh, was that supposed to be a secret, too?"

But Stone slipped his arm around her waist and gave her a little hug. His eyes were a riot of mirth that only she could see. "Darling, we don't have any secrets from my friends." He turned a fond gaze on Carolyn. "And Carolyn is a *very* old friend."

Carolyn looked as though she didn't know at all how to take that, and Stone didn't give her a chance to reply. He suddenly exclaimed, "Sweetheart, they're playing our song! Let's dance."

Allison was glad to leave Carolyn behind, and so, apparently, was Stone. As soon as they were out of earshot he burst into laughter. "Damn, we're good," he declared. "Let's find someone else and do it again."

"If I have to rescue you from another Carolyn I'm demanding overtime. What is she, an ex-girlfriend?"

"Of course not. My ex-girlfriends are much nicer."

"And what is this about our song? 'Wipe-Out' is our *song?* You couldn't have picked something more romantic?"

He draped his arm around her shoulders, his eyes twinkling. "Now aren't you having fun?"

Allison knew she shouldn't be. The entire purpose of this evening—or so she had convinced herself—was to cultivate Stone Harrison's goodwill and discuss the dinner party he had hired her to plan for his clients next month. So far she didn't even know what business he was in. As a matter of fact she didn't even know his real name. All she had managed to do so far was to lie to his mother and his ex-wife, antagonize an old friend by the name of Carolyn and pretend to a roomful of people that she was engaged to be married to a man she had known for less than two hours total. Somehow she did not think this was what Penny, or anyone else for that matter, would consider professional behavior.

But she was having fun.

She took a determined breath. "You know, you did say we were going to discuss business."

"Did I?" His hand moved in an absent fashion up and down her back as he escorted her through the crowd, and even though he was no doubt unaware of the caress, even though it was too impersonal to even be called a caress, his touch sent a tingle of awareness up and down her spine that was anything but impersonal.

She quickened her step a little, moving ahead of him. His hand fell away. She felt very virtuous as she continued firmly, "You certainly did. And I really think we ought to..."

He said, "One of the first things you'll have to learn about me is that I very often say things I don't mean, particularly if it makes it a little easier to get what I want."

She stopped and stared at him. "You mean you lie."

He pretended thoughtfulness. "A lie is really a relative thing. I prefer to think of it as manipulating the truth."

Allison looked at him dryly. "I have a feeling manipulating is something you do very well."

He returned a modest grin. "I practice at every opportunity."

Irresistible, she thought. She knew she should disapprove, as a woman, a businessperson and yes, even his coconspirator in crime, but found it almost impossible to do. He was irresistible.

He said, putting an end to the matter, "Business later, I promise. This is a party." Suddenly he cocked his head as the band struck up a different tune, his eyes glinting. "Say, do you tango?"

"Me?" She took a small, somewhat alarmed step backward. "Goodness, no, I—"

He caught her hand. "I'll teach you."

"But—"

He pulled her to him in one swift, dramatic gesture, his hand pressing hers down, his thigh cradling her hip, his eyes dancing wickedly above hers. "You, my dear," he declared, "are in for the time of your life."

He didn't lie about that. At two o'clock in the morning Allison sank back into the plush interior of the limousine, her head spinning, her muscles tingling, her head dancing with impressions from the evening. Other couples, on their way home or just out for a breath of air, called and waved to them and Allison returned their goodbyes, laughing, until the chauffeur closed the doors.

"Where did you learn all those strange dances?" she demanded, leaning her head back against the seat. "I'm exhausted! I didn't think anybody went to dance school anymore."

He made a small grimace. "You do if you belong to my mother. Ballroom dancing, age nine to twelve—till I got old enough to rebel and entered my famous punk stage. Of course in a few years I realized what a favor she'd done me. If all else fails I can always get a job as one of those gentlemen escorts on a cruise ship."

Allison laughed. "Punk stage? You?"

He unbuttoned his jacket so that he could comfortably rest his arm across the back of the seat, turning toward her. "After that I entered my even more infamous motorcycle gang stage. No, I'm serious—had a leather jacket and everything. It lasted about three months. I went through stages pretty fast."

It was difficult to imagine the sophisticated gentleman in the dinner jacket and black tie as ever having been anything so ordinary as a rebellious teenager in a leather jacket. The muted lights of passing cars and street lamps played across his face, softening his features, catching little sparks of fire in the depths of his eyes when he looked at her. His hair was tousled and damp where it curled over his forehead, the expanse of crisp white dress shirt beneath the casually unbuttoned jacket was oddly enticing. She could see the rise and fall of his chest in the shadowed interior of the car, and then she looked quickly away before he noticed her watching him.

She buried her face in the bridal bouquet and laughed softly. "Boy, are you going to have a lot of explaining to do Monday morning."

"I don't care. It was worth it." His lips curved into a slow smile, rich with memory. "God, it was perfect wasn't it? I couldn't have choreographed it better. And don't worry, I think I can talk those three fat women you knocked down trying to catch that thing out of suing."

"I did not!" She struck out at him playfully with the bouquet, and he chuckled.

"Perfect," he repeated. "Just perfect. Of course," he added, "you realize Melinda is a star pitcher with her women's softball team and she aimed right for you when she pitched that bouquet."

"I realize that she is pretty desperate to get you married and off her hands. But I don't care." She settled back into the deep upholstery, fingering the delicate petals of lace and hothouse flowers, then bringing it once again to her nostrils. "Catching the bouquet is good luck and I can use all the luck I can get."

"Can't we all?"

To her surprise, Stone let his hand drop, catching one of her curls and winding it around his finger playfully. "You should have taken a piece of wedding cake and slept with it under your pillow. Then you could have dreamed about the man you're going to marry."

She stared at him and he tugged her curl, looking smug. "I told you I knew about romance."

The motion of his fingers in her hair was soothing, his nearness mesmeric, the contentment of the evening infusive. She smiled drowsily. "I love weddings," she said with a sigh. She turned her head to look at him, and the motion resulted in his hand sliding down to cup the back of her neck. "That was what I originally intended Party Girls to be, you know—a wedding consultant and catering business. Of course that was before Penny gave it that stupid name—''

"Which sounds like another kind of business altogether."

"Exactly."

The warmth of his hand against her neck was wonderful, seeming to send out waves of pleasured awareness that matched the rhythms of her heartbeat. There was a light deep in his eyes that was hard to look away from; in contrast to that light his eyes looked almost black.

But Allison made herself look away. She swallowed hard and she said, "Speaking of business..."

He didn't move his hand—or perhaps he did. It seemed to Allison the pressure against her skin increased fractionally, but she could have imagined it. "We weren't, and we aren't going to. I have an appointment with you—or maybe it's your partner—sometime next week. We'll talk about it then."

She did not imagine the stroking motion of his two longest fingers against the back of her neck; it sent shivers down her spine. Nor did she imagine the slight increase of pressure that turned her head to face him, and she did not imagine that the light in his eyes had kindled to a low, soft flame. It made her breathing shallow.

The limousine glided to a stop. The moment between them hung suspended and rich and then Allison heard the driver's door close. She lowered her eyes. "I had a really great time tonight, Stone."

He smiled, and dropped his hand. "I'll walk you to your door."

The night air was chilly on her overheated skin, and she hugged her lace shawl to her as she fumbled in her evening purse for her keys. She wished the night didn't have to end. She wondered what Stone would say if she asked him in.

It took a couple of tries to get the key into the lock. *Don't be an idiot, Allison. Ask him in.* She turned to him, smiling apologetically. "I'd ask you in, but it's almost three in the morning..."

"And I need my beauty sleep." He handed her the bridal bouquet, which she had almost forgotten on the seat of the car. "Have I told you enough how much I appreciate what you did tonight? You were great."

Allison smiled. "You've mentioned it once or twice. Besides, I have to admit it was fun." Her smile faded as she added, "But you *will* tell your mother first thing in the morning? I'd feel awful if—"

"Done," he assured her. "Meanwhile..." He reached behind her and she thought he was going to open the door. Instead he rested his hand on the door panel near her shoulder. "I always pay my debts." He brought the other hand up to rest against the door panel on the other side of her shoulders, effectively trapping her with his nearness. He leaned closer; his thighs brushed, but did not press hers.

He kissed her.

It wasn't simply a kiss. It was a slow invasion, a warm consumption, a deft and thorough arousal of every sense she possessed. He didn't touch her. No part of his body made contact with hers except his mouth—first his lips, soft, warm, melting her resistance. Then his tongue, teasing, tantalizing and tasting. Then all of him, heat and moisture, a slow infiltration that swelled and expanded until no part of her—no cell, no nerve ending, no synaptic relay or neural fiber was left untouched. Her breath stopped in her throat, her heartbeat went wild. Her muscles sagged and her skin flamed and her head swam and that was only part of what he did to her. Her very brain pulsed to overflowing with awareness of him, and the pure, raw sexual ache he created within her from only his kiss was like nothing she had ever known.

Even after he lifted his face, the sensations lingered, the ache wouldn't fade. It was a moment before she could open her eyes; yet another, longer moment, before she regained her breath. She was leaning against the door on legs that were so rubbery she was surprised to find herself standing at all; his hands were still braced on either side of her shoulders. There was a faint flush to his skin and a slow burning fire in his eyes, the same kind of fire he had so expertly ignited within her. But his smile was gentle and his tone soft.

"Well?" he asked. "Did the world stop spinning?"

Allison had to press her hands against the door for support. Her knees still felt weak. She cleared her throat and replied, not too breathlessly, "More or less."

The smile deepened. "Good."

He didn't move, not closer, not farther away. His face filled her vision, his eyes encompassed her, her heart pounded with his closeness and her muscles ached with expectation. And slowly, he dropped his face closer to hers. His forehead rested against hers. She stopped breathing.

"Stonewall," he said softly. "It stands for Stonewall, after my great grandfather who fought with

General Stonewall Jackson." He straightened up, smiling. "Good night, Allison. It's been a pleasure."

He was halfway down the walk before Allison managed, somewhat dazedly, "Yes. It has."

Five

She tasted like mulled wine. Stone was still savoring that taste, remembering that kiss, at ten o'clock the next morning, and remembering was somewhat drugging...like a hangover without the unpleasant side effects. It bemused him and distracted him and was for all practical purposes a very annoying thing, yet he found himself deliberately replaying the memory, wanting the experience to linger. Stone was a person who lived very much in the present, if not the future, and to deliberate on something that had happened almost eight hours ago wasn't like him at all. Yet nothing about his behavior had been entirely typical since he'd met Allison Carter.

She enchanted him. Most women enchanted him, it was true, and he enjoyed each and every one with an open and unabashed thoroughness that was as much a part of his nature as breathing. But Allison was different. She had cast her spell and he had fallen under it willingly, but he knew from experience that it wouldn't last long. What would last—what puzzled him and delighted him and kept him turning pictures of her over in his mind long after he should have turned his attention to other matters—was that he liked her so much. He wanted to see her again.

Stone required very little sleep. He liked to think he had that in common with other mad geniuses and it was his custom to be in the office by six each morning, using those hours before the rest of the staff arrived as his most productive creative time. Despite the fact that he hadn't gotten to bed until after three, he had been at his desk that morning at the usual time. The only difference was that this morning a very small percentage of those hours had been neither productive nor creative.

As a general rule, Carla did not disturb him until noon. In return he did not disturb her with requests for coffee, freshly sharpened pencils or telephone numbers until the same hour. On a good day, in fact, he did not have to see anyone at all until he emerged for lunch. He therefore knew it was not going to be a particularly good day when the intercom buzzed, startling him out of his reverie. He also knew that whatever had prompted Carla to buzz him at this hour must be important.

He pushed the button but before he could form either a greeting or a reprimand Carla said crisply, "We have got to talk. But first, Mark Farmington is on Line One."

Mark Farmington was the American liaison for the Heroshito corporation. He and Stone had worked together quite closely over the past year and for that reason alone Carla would have put him through if he called at ten o'clock in the morning. What puzzled Stone was that he had no reason to be calling at all.

A good executive would have pushed the Connect button and taken matters firmly into his own hands. A lesser man would have asked his secretary what Mark wanted. Stone opened his mouth to question Carla, but she had already disconnected. He looked at the pulsing red light that represented Line One a moment longer, and then he pushed the button.

"Mark," he said, "it's good to hear from you." He leaned back in his chair and swung his feet up onto the desk, hoping that would reinforce the casualness he was trying to inject into his tone. "Last I heard you were in London. What's going on?"

Mark chuckled. "I could ask you the same thing. I hear congratulations are in order."

For a moment Stone literally did not know what he was talking about. By the time he understood, Mark was already speaking again.

"I'll tell you the truth, though, you could have saved me a lot of sleepless nights if you'd popped the question a little sooner. This isn't the same girl I met when I was in town last is it? What was her name?"

"Susan," Stone replied absently. "No, it's not. Listen, how did you hear about this anyway? And what do you mean about sleepless nights?"

"Do you remember Janet Wells from Logan and Price? I'm still working with her on the West Coast advertising contract, and when I spoke to her this morning..."

"Right," murmured Stone, still a little dazed. "Small world."

"I'll be frank with you, Stone," Mark said seriously, "this takes a load off my mind. As far as I'm concerned, you're the top bidder on the project. The next closest competition isn't even in your class."

Stone felt as though he had missed a big chunk of the conversation, and was already beginning to regret picking up the phone. He said carefully, "But?"

"But nothing. The Heroshito engineers were behind me all the way, so was the project planner, in fact the whole approval committee."

"Why do I think this story doesn't have a happy ending?"

"It does," Mark assured him quickly. "Now, it's just that...man, I really hate explaining this part."

"What?" Now that his dread had been somewhat assuaged, Stone let his curiosity take the front seat. "Should I start preparing myself for some ancient Oriental ritual?"

Mark chuckled, though it sounded a little uneasy. "Close, but only if you think of the marriage ceremony as an ancient ritual—and whether it's Oriental or not is purely optional."

Stone frowned, wondering if he was beginning to feel the effects of too much champagne and too little sleep. "What are you talking about?"

"It's hard for Americans to understand, coming from a totally different culture, and I guess that's part of my job, to bridge the gap. But whoever gets this contract will be very closely associated with Heroshito for quite some time—become a part of the corporate family, so to speak. And the company is very big on families, Stone. The truth is that the only thing that, as far as I can see, has ever stood in the way of your getting this contract was the fact that you were a single man.''

There was a moment in which Stone thought he might not have heard correctly. Mark interpreted his silence, more or less correctly, as simple astonishment.

"Yeah, I know," he said. "It sounds crazy but when you're as big as Heroshito you can make your own rules and one of them is that all the middle management and executive positions are filled by married men. If you think about it, it does make a twisted kind of business sense—"

"Whoa." At last Stone found his voice and, for good measure, he held up his hand in a blind gesture of protest. "Hold on just a minute, let me see if I've got this straight. Mine is the best bid on the project, right?"

"Right."

"But I probably won't get the job because I'm not *married?*"

"No, of course not. I'll admit it was a problem when you were going through women like other guys go through cheap socks, but now that you've decided to settle down and act like the responsible, upstanding young pillar of society we all know you can be—"

"In the first place," Stone interrupted firmly, "I'm *not* employed by Heroshito and I don't want to be. All I want is their money. They can't—"

"I'm afraid they can, my friend. They want their associates to be men of good character and in their minds that means a family man. The way they figure it, a married man is more stable, a man with a family depending on him has more invested in his own success. But there's no point in getting hot under the collar about it now. It's not a problem anymore. Although," he admitted with a slight chuckle, "if you were inclined to move the date up so that the deed would be done before they made a final decision on the contract it wouldn't hurt."

"In the second place," Stone said, and then stopped. He had been about to say *I'm not getting married,* and when he opened his mouth again he was quite sure that was what he intended to say. But the words that came out were, "This is the craziest thing I ever heard."

Again Mark chuckled. "Wait until you've been in this business awhile longer, then talk to me about crazy. Listen, we want to meet the lucky woman and drink a toast to both of you. Let me have Sarah call you and set something up for next week."

Stone replied absently, "Yeah, sure."

"And listen, Stone, if things go the way I expect next month when the planning committee is over here, this might not be the last time I'll be congratulating you."

When Stone hung up the phone he sat there for a minute, wondering whether or not this might, in some conceivable way, be traced back to one Miss Allison Carter's idea of a practical joke, but almost before he conceived it he dismissed the idea. No, this was real. It was entirely too bizarre not to be.

He was in deep trouble, and there was only one thing to do.

He leaned forward and punched the intercom button. "Carla," he ordered sharply. "Get my mother on the phone."

"Not Cinderella," Allison said. Her expression was musing as she cradled the coffee cup against her chest. "More like . . . do you remember the ball scene in *My Fair Lady?*"

Penny's eyes sparkled as she began to hum "I Could Have Danced All Night."

"Exactly." Allison couldn't seem to get rid of the dreamy smile that kept wanting to creep to her lips, even with a sip of Penny's brutally bad coffee. "Pure romance." Then she looked at her partner in muted alarm and corrected quickly, "Not that he and I—I mean, by romance I mean... You know what I mean."

"I know. And you're a sucker for it."

Allison mustered up a frown and hoped it disguised the sudden color in her cheeks, which was a direct result of the memory of the way Stone Harrison had said good-night. She gave a dismissive wave of her hand. "I am not," she said.

"Oh, yeah? Who else but a sucker for romance would think she could make a living planning weddings? And why do you think it is that when we *do* get a wedding I'm the one who wants to transport the wedding party on black motorcycles while you're the one who wants to wrap the spokes of the wedding carriage wheels in roses? I still think the motorcycles are a good idea, by the way," she added.

Allison grinned and took another sip of her coffee. "They must have ordered every salmon-colored rose in the city for that wedding," she remembered. "Of course if I had planned it I would have used white on white. There's a lot to be said for simplicity."

Penny grimaced. "White roses at a wedding? Too funereal."

"I like white roses." But she smiled as her eyes moved to the desk, whose corners were still flanked by two vases of roses. She was growing to like red roses, too. Not to mention yellow.

They had no appointments scheduled for the day, which was sadly not an uncommon state of affairs these days, and the atmosphere in the combination living room/office was relaxed. Penny, who would have dressed for work in high heels and a suit if her job had been that of garbage collector, had nonetheless arranged her crepe jacket on the back of her chair, discarded her heels and propped her stockinged feet up on the desk. Allison was more comfortable in an oversize, sloppy sweater and gray sweatpants, with her hair pinned in a random knot atop her head. Penny's arrival for work had awakened her that morning. And as far as Allison was concerned, her partner was lucky she had come downstairs at all; makeup and shoes were completely out of the question. She lay back on the sofa, propped up by pillows and sipping her coffee, while a morning talk show played softly on the television across the room. And whenever a new memory of the night before occurred to her she smiled.

Penny said, "Well for someone who was throwing such a tantrum about going, you sure lucked out. The food was great, the entertainment was great, you're a sucker for weddings anyway—"

"I am not!"

"You caught the bouquet!"

Allison shrugged a little uncomfortably. The *reason* she had caught the bouquet—the reason the bride had tossed it to her—was not something she wanted to go into at this hour of the morning.

"And you could have done a whole lot worse for a date," Penny concluded. "The man was walking sin in that dinner jacket. And that limo!"

"What were you doing, watching from the windows?"

Penny nodded vigorously. "You bet. After all the man's a client, I had to check him out. And boy did he check out!"

Allison couldn't help responding to that with a grin, nor could she argue with Penny's conclusions. "All right," she admitted. "It was fun. You were right. Next subject."

"So what did you find out about this job he wants us to do?"

Allison lowered her eyes to the coffee cup. "Well, about that..."

"You did say you were going to discuss business, didn't you?"

Allison lifted the cup to her lips to postpone the answer, and just then the telephone rang.

Penny swung her feet down from the desk, automatically assuming a professional pose as she answered the telephone. After a moment she held out the receiver to Allison. "Do you know a Mrs. Blake?"

"No." Allison's brow knit curiously as she sat up, reaching for the extension at the end of the sofa. "A client, maybe?"

"Or a collection agency."

It was with that thought in mind that Allison picked up the receiver and spoke into it warily. "This is Allison Carter, may I help you?"

"Allison." The voice on the other end was warm and instantly familiar. "This is Stella Blake, Gregory's—though he *will* insist on being called Stone—

mother. I do hope I'm not calling too early. It was a late night last evening, wasn't it?"

Allison's throat was so closed with surprise, and an uncertain, undefinable dread, that she could barely stammer the single word, "Y-yes."

"I can't tell you how devastated I am that we got to spend so little time together," Stella went on energetically. "How on earth did we ever get separated? Imagine, my son introduces his fiancée to his mother for the first time and we hardly say more than a half dozen words to each other!"

The dread sank into horror, and that horror was so miserable, so paralyzing, that she couldn't have spoken if she had wanted to. And the worst thing was that she didn't, for the longest time, even know what to say.

Stella Blake went on, cheerfully oblivious. "Well, I'm going to remedy that right now. Are you free for lunch? I know it's awfully short notice but the first thing you must learn about me is I'm dreadfuly impatient—a trait I may have passed on to my son, I'm afraid. We have so much to talk about and I simply can't wait another moment to learn all about you. Would one o'clock be convenient? I could call for you or—"

"Mrs. Blake." Allison felt as if she were a drowning woman coming up for air and she practically gasped the words.

"Stella, please."

"Stella." And then Allison found she didn't know what to say. She turned her eyes in mute appeal to Penny, but received only a blank look in return as she realized Penny had no way of guessing what was going on. As for Allison, she couldn't *believe* what was going on. Stone Harrison had not told his mother the truth. The rat had promised her and she had believed him but *he hadn't told her*.

Allison screwed up her courage, her fingers tightening on the receiver and blurted, "Stella, I'm afraid there's been a—a misunderstanding. I..."

And into the polite, inquiring silence on the other end of the phone Allison found she could not go on. How could she tell this perfectly harmless woman— this woman who had hugged her so warmly, whose eyes had filled with happy tears at the belief her son was engaged—how could she blurt out to her over the phone that she had been nothing more than the victim of a practical joke? As much as she wanted to blame Stone for this—and he was at least fifty percent culpable—it had been Allison who had told the lie in the first place. At the very least she should face the wronged party in person and make her apologies.

As the silence lengthened, Stella said, "My gracious. I have called at a bad time haven't I?"

"No," Allison said quickly. "No, not at all. That is, I..." And she had no choice. She steeled herself with resignation for what would undoubtedly be the worst ordeal of her life. "I'd love to meet you for lunch."

"Wonderful. Do you know Stephanie's? One o'clock?"

Allison assured her that would be fine, and hung up the phone with leaden fingers.

"Good Lord, who was that?" Penny inquired. "You look like somebody just invited you to a lynching."

"Someone did," Allison replied dully. "My own."

She swallowed hard and raised stricken eyes to her friend. "Oh, Penny," she said. "I am in such trouble."

Six

Allison spent the next two hours alternately trying to reach Stone and inventing cowardly and increasingly imaginative excuses not to keep the appointment with his mother. Stone himself had been too afraid to tell her the truth. Why should Allison step in to do his dirty work? She was furious with him and if she had been able to reach him she would have been happy to tell him exactly what she thought of his brand of gallantry, but Stone Harrison was either genuinely out of the office or not accepting her calls.

And in the end Allison knew, as she had truthfully known all along, that there was nothing to do but set her teeth and face the music. She had done something foolish and she had gotten caught. Now she had to pay the price. It was as simple as that.

But that did not keep her from plotting more and more gruesome revenges on Stone Harrison.

Penny was a firm believer in the adage "clothes make the woman," and had, therefore, insisted that Allison gird herself for battle in brilliant colors. Her philosophy was that it was impossible to be timid while wearing bright yellow city shorts and a matching jacket, with a four-foot purple-and-red print scarf pinned to one shoulder. Allison was not at all sure how much the bold outfit did for her courage, but it certainly made it impossible to change her mind once she walked into the restaurant. Stella Blake spotted her immediately from a window table, and raised her hand to beckon her over.

Allison swallowed hard, squared her shoulders and made her way over to the table. She didn't even try to smile. There was no reason to postpone the inevitable with a lot of politeness.

Allison did not sit down. She doubted she'd be welcome after she finished what she had to say. She drew a breath and began firmly, "Mrs. Blake—"

"Stella, for heaven's sake." The other woman grasped her hand and squeezed it warmly. "And you may feel free to sit down. I promise I won't bite."

There was a twinkle in her eyes that reminded Allison suddenly, poignantly of her son, and with that reminder came a muffled suspicion—just enough to make her obey the other woman's invitation and sink cautiously into a chair. Before Allison could resume her carefully rehearsed speech, Stella waved her silent, assuming a brisk and businesslike tone.

"We have a great deal to discuss and very little time in which to do it," she said. "First of all, relax for heaven's sake. I know you're not engaged to my son, never have been and at this point most probably have no intention of ever becoming so, although I do reserve the right to reopen that subject at a later date. I apologize for any undue anxiety I've caused you but frankly, I suspected the only way you'd keep this appointment was if you thought you owed me an explanation in person, and I *did* think it was important that we meet.''

All the air went out of Allison's lungs in a gasp and she stared at the other woman limply. ''But—but how...I didn't think Stone—''

Again she made a dismissive gesture, this time accompanied by a small grimace. ''I knew from almost the first moment, my dear. I've known the boy for thirty-two years and he's never once been able to successfuly lie to me. And although I'll give you credit for deceiving me for the first couple of moments, which isn't easily done I'll assure you...'' She lifted her glass and her eyes moved over Allison in a very clinical way. ''I must confess anyone can see you're not really Gregory's type. Of course,'' she added, and sipped from the glass. ''My son did have the courtesy to call this morning and confirm my suspicions. Even though his motives were somewhat less than altruistic, I will admit he was moved to honesty in the end.''

Allison not only did not know what to say, but she didn't even know what to think, and what she felt was quite simply stunned. She knew she should be upset with the other woman's manipulations, but she was too relieved. She supposed she should have been grateful that Stone had, in fact, kept his promise even at the last minute and confessed to his part in the duplicity, but she was too annoyed with him for all the trouble he had caused to feel much of anything beyond that. She couldn't begin to guess why Stella had called her here—except for the satisfaction of seeing

Allison's embarrassment as her deception was exposed, which she certainly deserved—but she had to assume the interview was over.

She cleared her throat a little and gathered the straps of her purse together in preparation for rising. She said, "I don't know how to apologize. What I did was completely out of line and I'm just glad no one was hurt by it. I'm usually not like that, really, and I don't have any excuse except..." She looked at her with the frankness of heartfelt regret and finished, somewhat lamely, "It was just a crazy impulse and I didn't know you were his mother."

Stella Blake burst into laughter. She had a full, uninhibited laugh that was loud enough to make heads turn and bold enough to make perfect strangers smile indulgently before they looked away. Allison didn't know whether to sink into her chair and await further reprimands or mumble a final apology and make her escape while she still could.

As though reading her mind, Stella reached across the table and laid her hand atop Allison's, letting the laughter fade to chuckles as she declared, "There, you see! *That's* why I wanted to meet you. Quick *and* honest, not to mention that dash of integrity that's so hard to find these days. You'll do," she decided, and the narrowing of her eyes was not so much shrewd as affectionate, "You'll do very nicely indeed."

Stella gave Allison's hand one last pat before returning to her drink, and Allison said hesitantly, "I'm glad you're not angry. But I'm afraid I don't understand—"

"No, of course you don't, and I doubt you will even after I've explained it. But what a bad hostess I am. I haven't even given you a chance to order." She finished her drink and lifted her hand for the waiter's attention. "The food here is really quite pedestrian," she confided, "but nourishing enough I suppose, and the dessert tray is worth waiting for. I recommend a light soup and salad, and we'll have something sinful to finish."

Against all reason—for Allison certainly had reason to be uneasy around the other woman, if not actually wary—she found herself liking Stella Blake a great deal. By the time they had given their orders to the waiter Allison was almost comfortable, despite the fact that she still had no idea why she was here and wasn't entirely sure she wanted to know.

When the waiter was gone Stella settled back and began without preamble, "First I want to make it clear that my presence here today should in no way be taken as an endorsement of my son's actions. He's a presumptuous young man who in my opinion gets away with far too much as it is, and the last thing I want is that you should feel any pressure from me. However..."

Allison, who had taken a sip of water, had to swallow quickly. Even through her confusion, she could tell the discourse was about to take a turn she wouldn't like. "Excuse me, but what has Stone done? And what has it got to do with me?"

"It's not what he's done, but what he is about to do. As for what it has to do with you..." She leaned back and regarded Allison in a friendly manner. "That's all up to you, isn't it?"

Allison gave a little shake of her head, forcing a bewildered smile. "I'm afraid I'm lost."

"I will say this," Stella announced abruptly, "I'm sorry this engagement of yours was only a joke and I won't make any bones about it now or later. You got the best of him last night—maybe for only a second or two, but you did it, and that's something no woman before you has ever been able to do. For that I applaud you. Furthermore, I'd like to go on record as saying I can't think of a reason in the world you should help him out of a mess that, as far as I can tell, he got himself into. However . . ." And her eyes took on that twinkle again, the one that was so very much like Stone's. "If you think about it a moment, I think you'll find the opportunity that's about to be offered you has possibilities that are almost too good to turn down."

Allison took another sip of water, forcing back uneasiness. But she couldn't help remembering the last "opportunity" Stone Harrison had offered her, and she murmured, "Somehow I have a feeling I'm *really* not going to like this."

"Nonsense," Stella said briskly. "Every woman has a secret ambition to tame the beast—and I think you'll agree my Gregory needs a great deal of taming."

And then, as though to fend off a polite protest Allison had no intention of making, Stella lifted her hand and added airily, "Oh, I know, he's very urbane and civilized and he does have a certain surface charm even I find difficult to resist, but when it comes to genuine human relationships he is a hopeless case. You wanted to teach him a lesson, didn't you? Well, it's going to take more than one evening to teach the kind of lessons Gregory needs to learn. And very few women will ever have the chance you are about to be given."

Allison was almost certain she wasn't going to like this. "I really don't think . . ."

"Not that I'd blame you if you walked out of here and never looked back. In fact if I were in your place I'm quite sure that's exactly what I would do. But keep in mind that if you do that he'll only find someone else, and all that would prove is that he is very adept at getting his own way—a concept that I frankly don't think needs any more reinforcing. So think about it, my dear, and whatever you decide rest assured you have my full support."

There was a great deal Allison would have liked to say then—beginning with a plain and graceless demand to know what, exactly, the other woman was talking about—but when she opened her mouth no words came out. In fact, no breath came out, either, because when she looked over Stella's shoulder what she saw momentarily froze her in place.

Stone moved across the room with the easy grace of natural confidence that Allison recalled so well from the night before. He was wearing a pearl-gray shirt with the sleeves rolled up and the collar unbuttoned, and a tie so loosely knotted that it looked as though it had been pulled on over his head. He wore black jeans and running shoes. His hair was windblown and his jaw faintly stubbled, and female heads turned when he passed.

He came up behind his mother and dropped a kiss on her cheek. His eyes met Allison's and she couldn't help it—all she could think about was the breath robbing, mind-scrambling, muscle-melting effect of his kiss, and remembering made her cheeks warm. Worse, in that first instant when their eyes met she was convinced he was remembering the same thing, and she was uncomfortable and irritated. Men who were that skillful should have the good grace not to go around reminding women by look, touch or word, how thoroughly susceptible said women were to their charms.

Stella said impatiently, "You're early, as usual. Where on earth you got your abhorrent sense of timing I can't imagine. Well, you may as well sit down. I hope you've eaten," she added as she saw the waiter approaching, "because we've already ordered and we're not going to wait for you."

Stone smiled at his mother, and said, "Hello, Allison. Thanks for coming."

It was at that point that Allison realized two things: she had been nicely manipulated into a situation from which she could not possibly emerge a winner, and this might well be her last chance to walk away.

She told herself that the only reason she remained seated was that the waiter chose that moment to serve the soup.

Stone took the seat between Allison and his mother and ordered a club soda. When the waiter was gone he turned to Allison and said, "I guess Mother explained the situation to you."

"I most certainly did not," replied his mother disdainfully. "I told you from the outset I disapproved of your little scheme and I certainly can't be expected to do your dirty work for you. Aside from that, you're far too old to be running to your mother every time you get into trouble."

The corners of Stone's mouth turned down dryly. "Thank you, Mother. You're exactly what a man needs when he's trying to build confidence with a young lady." He turned to Allison. "For the record, the only reason I called her at all was that I promised you I would . . ."

"And to get my reaction to your plan," his mother pointed out.

Allison tasted her soup.

"All right, I admit I wanted a woman's opinion. And," he continued, speaking to Allison, "when she said she wanted to have lunch with you anyway—"

"I said you might come by for dessert."

"The reason I'm early is to try to prevent you from doing any more damage than absolutely necessary, but I see I'm too late. Allison's not even speaking to me," he pointed out.

"Which already proves she has more sense than the average woman." Stella picked up her spoon. "How's the soup, my dear?"

"Quite good," Allison replied pleasantly.

The waiter brought Stone's club soda. Out of the corner of her eye, Allison watched as his fingers curved around the glass—long, slender fingers, strong wrists lightly sprinkled with gold-brown hairs, deft magician's hands that could manipulate a woman's body as effortlessly as his silver tongue and easy charm could manipulate her emotions.

Allison quickly forced her attention back to the soup but it had lost its flavor. Her pulse was beating just the slightest bit faster, and her cheeks were beginning to warm. She reached for her water, and when Stone began to speak she did not dare look at him.

Stone said resolutely, "It's like this. I'm bidding on a job—the biggest I've ever done, certainly the most prestigious. I've been working on it for over a year. The company is owned by the Japanese—those are the people you were going to help me entertain when they came to town next month, remember?"

The waiter brought the salads, and Allison smiled at him, deliberately avoiding Stone's gaze. One look at those smoky-gray eyes and she would be drawn into whatever tale he was spinning, helpless to refuse his most outrageous demands.

He said, "The thing is, these people have some rather peculiar ideas about what qualifies someone to work with them. They only hire married executives, and it seems they like to apply the same kind of criteria to the people they do business with on a long-term basis. The truth is, even though mine was the best bid, I wasn't even under consideration for the project until this morning, when word got back to them that I was engaged to be married . . . to you."

With a very great effort, Allison managed not to drop her fork, but she could not prevent her gaze from rising slowly to meet his. As hard as she searched for some sign of mischief or deception there all she saw was sobriety—and perhaps just the faintest trace of puzzled anxiety, as though he could not quite believe the turn of events himself. She moved her gaze from Stone to his mother, but that woman was enjoying her salad and appeared to be disinterested in what was going on around her.

"I know it started out as a joke, Allison." Stone went on. "But I guess we were too good at it, and we convinced too many people. Now it's started to backfire."

There it is, Allison thought, *the guilt.* She knew she was lost. She never should have looked at him. Deliberately, she turned back to her salad.

"So what I'm getting at is this. If we could keep it up for another month or so—just until after I get the contract—that's all it would be. Then we could have a lover's quarrel and break up and no one need ever be the wiser.''

Allison stabbed at a cherry tomato and missed. The fork made a sharp clink against the plate but from that table there was no other sound.

Into her silence Stone said simply, ''Well, I guess that's about it. What do you think? You probably have some questions.''

Allison put her fork down carefully, and touched her napkin to her lips. ''Just one.''

He waited.

''Who's paying for lunch?''

Stone blinked once. ''I am.''

''In that case...'' Allison picked up her fork again. ''I think I will have dessert after all.''

Across the table from her, Stella chuckled. ''Well done, my dear.''

Stone glared at her.

''Of course,'' he continued carefully, ''it's not as though you'd really have to do anything—just don't correct anyone who's under the impression that we're engaged if you should happen to meet them on the street. Just play the role for a week or so next month while the Heroshito people are in town, and on one or two social occasions where you'd have to attend as my fiancée. But I won't offer to pay you for that,'' he assured her hastily. ''I know how you feel about turning personal favors into business transactions.''

There were a great many responses she could have made to that, ranging from the merest observation that *she* would prefer to decide for what she should and should not be paid, to an incredulous demand as to what right he had to be asking her any favors at all. She knew that neither of those remarks would be either useful or effective, however, so she settled for a murmured, "At least you're a fast learner," and she tried to force down another bite of lettuce.

"But," he went, "I realize this problem isn't entirely your fault—"

At that, Allison couldn't prevent a shocked, incredulous look, which he completely ignored.

"—And I don't expect you to inconvenience yourself for nothing. After all, I'll be getting a contract out of it and I think you should have some kind of compensation."

His mother, who had shown admirable restraint in staying out of the conversation so far, put in dryly, "Don't you mean *inducement,* my dear?"

Stone ignored her as easily as he had ignored Allison's incredulity a moment earlier. He reached into his pocket and took out a folded paper. "I had my secretary make some calls this morning. These are people who could use a service like yours and who incidentally owe me a favor."

Allison said, "You don't even know what our service does."

"No," he admitted, "not entirely. But my secretary does, and she's the one who made up the list. The jobs are yours if you want them."

He offered the paper to her and Allison hesitated, feeling like Persephone in the Underworld. For that unfortunate lady it had been a handful of pomegranate seeds that had sealed her fate. For Allison it was the contents of that list. If she looked she would be lost.

She took the list.

There were perhaps half a dozen names there. Not a single recording artist, personal manager or movie star was there. But Allison kept her own list in her head and she recognized some of the most successful men and women in the city—a real estate broker, a developer, a computer wizard. And beside each name was a date and a small notation: "Anniversary," "Sweet Sixteen," "Retirement," "Awards Banquet." They were genuine jobs. Moreover they were important jobs, solid contacts, the kind of jobs Allison had been trying to get since she started the company. It was the closest thing Allison had ever received to an offer she couldn't refuse.

The silence grew heavy as she stared at the paper and Stone waited for her reply. Stella broke in at last by placing her napkin beside her plate and announcing, "Well, as curious as I am to see how this all turns out, I can see my work here is done." She leaned across to pat Allison's hand and added, "You see, my dear, he is quite incorrigible. You have your work cut out for you. As for you," she told Stone as she stood, "I am forgoing dessert for your sake and I *do* expect to be compensated. And don't overtip, dear," she added, giving his shoulder a brief caress in passing. "The service was only mediocre."

Allison followed her departure with a somewhat dazed expression, and then she turned back to Stone. They looked at each other for a long time. Then Allison said, "I'm beginning to understand what you meant."

"About my family?"

Such was the strangeness of the entire episode that Allison didn't find it at all odd that he should understand immediately to what she referred. She nodded.

He said, "My father owned a circus."

She was almost tempted to comment on that. She thought better of it just in time. Instead she glanced down at the list in her hand. She cleared her throat. "Stone..."

He said quickly, "I want you to know I *didn't* ask her to help. In the first place, she wouldn't have done it and in the second anything she could have said to you about me would have only made things worse."

Allison smiled. "You do have an interesting relationship. But Stone..."

He said quietly, "It's really important to me, Allison."

There were a dozen things he could have said, a hundred, and at least as many things he could have done. But that simple statement was all it took because she looked into his eyes and she knew that for perhaps the first time since she had met him he was telling her the plain unvarnished truth. It was not only important to him, but it was the most important thing in his life. And he was trusting her with it.

She glanced down at the paper in her hand, looked back at him. She could not entirely stifle a helpless little sigh. "Just one question."

He seemed to relax a fraction. "What's that?"

"What is it that you *do?*" she asked.

A slow, delighted grin spread over his face, and his eyes sparkled. He caught her hand. "Come on," he said, tugging her from her chair. "I'll show you."

Seven

"Somebody owes me dessert," Allison complained as Stone swept her past his staring secretary and into his private office. But the complaint was far from heartfelt. She felt as though she were a child on the verge of an adventure, for Stone's enthusiasm was that contagious. His touch, however casual it might be, was electric, and without even knowing what it was he was about to show her she felt privileged to be chosen to view it—or perhaps that was a natural reaction to being with Stone.

"A demonstration wasn't called for, you know," she added. "A simple one-sentence answer would have sufficed. I would have believed you."

He chuckled, and closed the door behind them. "No, you wouldn't."

She remembered the office from their first interview. Everything about that encounter was etched in-

delibly on her mind: the gracious use of chrome and
obsidian, black and gray, light and dark. There was a
bank of what appeared to be built-in cabinets on one
wall with smoked-glass fronts. She assumed they con-
cealed an entertainment center or a wet bar or both.
The wall behind Stone's desk was composed mainly of
windows, and when he stepped behind the desk and
pushed a button electric shutters descended—black of
course—sealing the room and leaving it illuminated
only by soft recessed spots.

He came around the desk again and took Allison's
hand, leading her a few steps forward to the center of
the room and then, settling his hands on her shoulders, turned her toward the banks of smoked-glass
cabinets. "Stay there," he ordered. "Don't move."

He returned to the desk and Allison watched in
amazement as with another touch of a button the glass
top parted and a computer monitor ascended from a
recessed alcove beneath it. A small shiver of anticipation—or perhaps apprehension—went through Allison as she waited obediently in the center of the
room. The soft lighting shaded Stone's face into deep
planes of intense concentration, his fingers flew across
the keyboard with all the mastery of a concert musi-
cian, and suddenly he was a stranger to her—starkly
handsome, distant and mysterious, absorbed in a
world of his own creating.

But his voice was the same, easy and familiar.
"You're not afraid of the dark, are you?"

She couldn't prevent an uneasy glance toward the
door. "No, of course not. What—"

Suddenly the room went black.

Allison wasn't afraid of the dark, she really wasn't.
But there was a difference between ordinary darkness

and this sudden, complete blackness, locked in an unfamiliar room with no landmark from which to get her bearings. Even the muffled tap of the keyboard had stopped and she didn't know where Stone was. For all she knew he could have left her completely alone. She forced herself to stand perfectly still. She strained her eyes in the dark and tried, very hard, to keep her voice steady. "Stone..."

"Look up," he said softly.

Allison could not tell from which direction his voice came and there was something strangely thrilling about that—reassuring, because she wasn't alone, yet disturbing, because she didn't know what he had in mind for her. And even though she knew it was all calculated for effect—the darkness, the disembodied voice—that did not prevent the small shiver from tantalizing her spine.

She tilted her head back, looking up toward the ceiling and she gasped. The roof had opened onto a rich nighttime sky, a vast midnight blue crowded with stars so brilliant she wanted to lift her hand and grasp a pocketful. Once she had seen a sky like that on a clear night in the desert—it had taken her breath away then as it did now. Hardly had she begun to absorb the miracle of this before the most extraordinary thing happened. She felt the gust of a breeze on her cheek. The stars, incredibly, seemed to be moving. Then she realized it wasn't the stars but the floor on which she stood that was moving, gaining acceleration, moving forward and upward toward the sky. She cried out and flung out her arms for balance and felt Stone's arms come around her from behind, drawing her back against him.

"It's okay, I've got you," he said. "Watch."

His arms were firm around her waist and his stance was steady. After a moment Allison relaxed enough to drop her hands to his arms, holding on to him lightly, and to tilt her head back toward the stars again. The wind was streaming past her face now, blowing her hair back, raising gooseflesh on her exposed skin. The night sky spread around them until they were standing—no, flying through the darkness of space and the blur of starlight. Allison's heartbeat was similar to a series of stuttering explosions deep in her chest. She couldn't get her breath and her fingers dug into Stone's arms. And though she wanted to squeal like a child on a roller coaster with that thrilling, primal combination of fear and delight, she couldn't manage a sound. She was lost in wonder, completely absorbed by the experience, terrified and thrilled and captivated and excited. She held on to Stone for dear life and gasped out loud with amazement.

And then speed seemed to slow, and the wind faded from a stinging stream to a steady flow to rising and falling gusts. The blurs of light that once had been stars now coalesced slowly into planetary shapes— weird, otherworldly colors and gauzy atmospheres and strangely arranged landmasses—that drifted past Allison's range of vision like clouds past an airplane window... only there was no window and no airplane and it was she who was drifting weightless through space. She and Stone, holding on to each other while worlds passed them by.

The movement gradually ceased and they appeared to be standing on the surface of an alien planet. A rust-colored sky swirled around them, lit by the glow of a scarlet sun in the distance. Allison could feel the heat of that sun on her right cheek. In the east hung two orange moons, one slightly above the other. Smoky darkness whirled around her feet but when she looked straight ahead she could see the undulating sands of purple dunes and rich, golden desert. The air was hot and dry and it smelled like ancient parchment, crisp and dry, like sun-baked stone, from centuries and centuries of desert heat. Distinctly alien. Distinctly real.

She whispered, "My God. You're a magician."

She could hear the smile in his voice. "No. Just an engineer. Welcome to Celiton Three, my little home away from home."

Now that the sensation of motion was gone, Allison's fingers relaxed their death-grip on Stone's arms, but she could not entirely let him go. For one thing, the sense of disorientation was still so strong that she wasn't entirely sure that if she left the protective circle of Stone's arms she wouldn't literally fall off the edge of the world. The heat of the sun on her cheek, the taste of the air, the shifting, pulsating, whirling colors of an alien sky. She knew they couldn't possibly be real, and yet the illusion was so perfect her heart pounded with the thrill of it. Her throat was dry with wonder and her senses simply refused to accept what her mind told her could not possibly be true. For another thing, she didn't want to leave the circle of Stone's arms.

At some point during the journey she had been drawn back completely against him—her head resting on his shoulder, her backside pressed into the cradle of his pelvis, his thighs strong and warm against hers. His body heat enfolded her, adding to the radiant glow of the air that surrounded them, but it wasn't an uncomfortable, feverish heat—it was more like the heat of a tanning bed or a sun-drenched beach, infusing, penetrating, inundating. She could feel his heartbeat, a strong steady pulse that seemed to capture the rhythm of this alien place, and the movement of his chest with each slow breath. His scent of wild herbs and grasses, mixed with that dry-hot smell of alien soil was strangely compelling, subtly erotic.

She drew in that scent in one long, slow breath, and heat seemed to melt into her muscles, causing her to sink further into his embrace. His nearness was almost as dizzying as the plummet through space had been, the only real and solid thing in this wild and thrilling place. Yet he, as its creator, was just as thrilling, more than a little wild.

She spoke, trying to anchor herself to reality before all that she knew—even her own good sense—slipped away. "We never left the office, did we?" Her voice sounded a little breathless.

"I'm not going to tell you." He spoke close to her ear, his breath causing a little tingle to play across the back of her neck. Again, she could hear, rather than see, his smile. "The trick to good illusion, my dear, is to make sure you never see the wires."

When he spoke his breath stirred a strand of hair that had been disarranged by the wind. Perhaps it tickled his face because he lifted his hand to smooth it back behind her ear. A perfectly innocent gesture, but then it wasn't. His fingers lingered against her skin, spreading slowly over the side of her face with a light and feathery caress, drawing pictures in the dark with touch alone. Her breath quickened as his fingertips followed the curve of her jaw, and moved upward behind her earlobes, discovering the sensitive spot there with a whispery caress that held just long enough to tantalize. The fingers of his other hand opened on her rib cage, the curve between the thumb and forefinger resting just beneath her left breast, forming a perfect cradle for the weight of her breast yet not touching.

He drew a breath, long and slow, his chest expanding against her back. His muscles stretched and rippled against her skin in a low, sensual unfolding that enveloped her with heat texture. She could feel his heartbeat and it was faster now, almost matching the rhythm of her own. The breath he released was somewhat unsteady as her fingers moved lightly across his arm, tracing the bone and muscle and the feathering of hair—golden-brown hair, she remembered, his skin as warm as sunshine.

A hot breeze gusted, bringing a brief intensity of that wild alien scent and drying the perspiration that, until that moment, Allison had not realized filmed her face. His fingertips moved in a maddening, wonderful caress from her ear to her collarbone, then nestled gently in the curve of her neck. Her attention was focused with aching intensity on the position of his other hand and she tried to control the shallow rhythm of her breathing as his hand moved at last, not upward, but down. His breath fanned slow and soft against the back of her neck, his lips so close she could practically feel their caress, yet never touching. His fingers spread across her rib cage, stroking delicately across her waist, drifting below, opening across her abdomen. The slow, firm pressure of his hand against her stomach was gentle and deliberate, causing the ache inside her to blossom and spread, weakening the strong muscles of her thighs, robbing her of breath completely. Colors whirled, a hot wind rose and the distant thunder that roared in her ears was their combined heartbeats. Without even trying he could do this to her, reducing her to a mindless mass of aching need from nothing more than a touch.

And yet she knew the change that came over him was deliberate and accomplished with a determined effort of will. Around them the rust sky darkened, fog billowed up from beneath their feet and obscured the unearthly landscape before them. The air took on the sharp taste of ozone. The muscles that were hard against Allison's back relaxed slowly and one by one, the pressure against her abdomen eased, the whisper of his breath, hot and damp, slowed and then moved away. With a reluctance that was apparent in every movement, he took a step away from her, moving his hands to rest lightly on either side of her waist.

By the time the fog cleared—both from her brain and from her literal surroundings—Allison realized that the scene around them had shifted. The opposite wall appeared now to be formed of stone, so perfect in every detail that she could see the moss and lichen that clung to the ancient mortar. In the center, flanked on either side by flickering pitch torches, was an enormous open door. Three times as tall as a man and twice as wide, it was a black, yawning orifice that seemed to take up most of what she remembered of that part of the room and lead to who knew what—if anything at all.

"My...goodness," she managed to say, and the wonder almost, though not quite, mitigated the disappointment she felt at the absence of Stone's warmth. The air around them now had a distinct chill and a touch of dampness.

"Go on," Stone urged with a slight pressure of his hands on her waist. "Walk toward it."

Allison glanced down and saw a path had been illuminated with an orangish light that might have been a reflection from the torches. Gradually she became aware of sounds in the background, such as the lapping of water, the muted croak of frogs. They appeared to be standing on a bridge. And the bridge was over a moat.

She shook her head adamantly. "There's nothing there. I'll walk into a wall."

"No, you won't," he insisted. Again he applied a slight forward pressure to her waist. "Trust me."

Trusting him, she realized instinctively, would never be a smart thing to do. She had trusted him when he turned out the lights and her head was still spinning. She had trusted him when he put his arms around her to keep her from falling, and she had only fallen— hard—in an entirely different direction. Where might he be leading her now?

She swallowed hard. "You go first."

"I can't. There's not enough room for me to get around you—I'll fall into the water."

Allison twisted her head around to look at him, but his face was just a shadow among shadows. Her mouth turned down dryly. "You know perfectly well there's nothing beneath your feet except floor."

And he replied blandly, "Isn't there?"

She took a cautious step forward, then another. He kept his hands on her waist as though to guide her, matching her hesitant, shuffling steps. The gaping door loomed ever closer, the flickering torches cast eerie dancing shadows across Allison's outstretched arm, and she couldn't shake the feeling that there was something terribly familiar about the entire scene—the rock wall, the huge door, the sound of lapping water and the dancing orange shadows. They were directly in front of the door now, close enough that she could feel the breath of dank, cool air that seemed to be emanating from somewhere inside. She stretched out her hand, pushing it cautiously against the blackness, expecting to feel the smooth glass cabinet front against her palm. She was so startled when she met no resistance at all and stumbled forward. Only Stone's hands on her waist kept her from falling to one knee.

She turned a startled glance on him, and his expression, illuminated by the rather ghoulish orange torch overhead, was perfectly innocent. "Go ahead," he invited. "It's safe."

Allison held her breath, and stepped through the door.

As she stepped inside, an unseen rheostat turned up the illumination, and she found herself standing in a narrow stone corridor. Water dripped audibly from an unknown source and the air smelled like the inside of a tomb. Before her was a sharply descending spiral staircase, around her a phalanx of torches, the stones behind them blackened with soot. To her direct right was a portrait, badly done in flat dull colors, of a man in Elizabethan dress with a pale face and piercing black eyes. Suddenly she remembered why it all seemed so familiar.

"Why," she exclaimed, "this is just like the Castle of Horrors in Yesteryear Park in Modesto! I was there just last year, when my nephew was out for a visit."

Stone stepped into the dim light beside her, smiling. "Did you have a good time?"

"Fabulous!" she enthused. "You wouldn't believe the rides they have. Talk about state-of-the-art technology! And the exhibits—"

She broke off as understanding slowly dawned. "Of course," she said softly, "you build castles. This isn't just *like* the Castle of Horrors..."

"It *is* the Castle of Horrors from Yesteryear Park," he admitted. "Or at least the most important rooms of it. This was the first full-scale prototype I built on site and I'm still finding ways to improve it." He moved in front of her. "I'll go first down the stairs. They're pretty narrow and can be a little tricky. Naturally we used a wider staircase in Modesto. Hold on to the rail."

But he had already descended three of the stairs before Allison recovered her presence of mind enough to follow him. She gripped the rail with both hands as she started quickly down the stone stairs. "You mean— this is what you do? Build amusement parks?"

"Theme parks," he corrected. "And no, I don't build them, I just design them, and usually not the whole park, just certain components. I come up with the concept for a haunted castle like this, or a ride like 'Undersea Adventure' in Three Islands Park in Hawaii. Have you been there?"

He glanced up at her and Allison shook her head, still hurrying to keep up as the staircase wound deeper and deeper into the darkness. His voice echoed off the damp walls in counterrhythm to the clatter of his footsteps as he went on. "It's something to see— you're in a glass submarine, actually about six feet underwater although of course it feels much deeper, you're chased by a Great White, attacked by a giant octopus and fall off the edge of the Cayman Trough— a two-mile free-fall, where you're saved from a pressure implosion at the last minute by a robotic submersible. I'm telling you, it's the ride of your life."

Allison nodded dazedly. "I've heard of it. And you invented it?"

"More or less. Of course I have a little help from my staff..." He reached out and the wall at Allison's elbow suddenly dissolved into a windowpane beyond which several men and women were moving around a room, working at drawing boards or at long tables, completely oblivious to the two who observed them from a castle on the other side of the wall. The disorientation was so intense that Allison stumbled and almost lost her balance.

"George there," Stone said, "was with NASA before he joined us—an electronics wizard. And if there's anything about lasers and holography Meg Robins doesn't know it's not worth knowing."

The window faded back into the wall and he continued to move downward. Allison followed carefully. "Now Ted and Franklin, they're the animation experts." Another window opened up, this time illuminating the somewhat startling sight of a huge lizard—no, dragon, Allison realized—lying on its side with its belly open to reveal a network of electronic boards and cables. One man crawled around inside with a screwdriver while another one perched on the dragon's shoulder, pushing the buttons of something that looked like an electric calculator. If Allison had not by then been so immune to the unexpected, she might very well have lost her footing with surprise.

"And of course here—" another window appeared, lower down "—is the heartbeat of the operation—research and development. If we need to know what kind of material was used for ladies' slippers in 1560, these guys find out. If we need to know what the wind velocity is on a planet a half dozen light years away, they'll calculate it. They review the plans and specs every step of the way and if it's not workable they find a way to make it work. So you see this is not exactly what you'd call a one-man operation."

"No," Allison murmured, as dazzled by all that she had seen behind the windows as she had been by the effects of their artistry on the upper levels. "I never even knew there *was* a business like this. And all of it for theme parks?"

"Most of it. Sometimes we'll free-lance a movie set or co-opt with one of the f/x outfits, but our services are pretty expensive."

"F/x," Allison repeated hesitantly. "Special effects? As in the movies?"

He tossed a grin up at her. "Right."

It might have been the effect of that grin, or it might have been the fact that he chose that moment to push the button that hid the last window, leaving the staircase illuminated only by the eerie, unsteady torchlight. The inevitable happened and Allison lost her footing. With a muffled cry, she plunged down into the darkness.

Stone caught her with a sweep of his arm, thrusting her back against the wall. The momentum swung him against her, pinning her between the wall and his body. For a moment they simply stared at each other, breathing hard with the quick adrenaline of alarm and relief. And then Allison realized that neither one of them was going to move away.

Stone's thighs were strong against hers, his chest a hard, warm pressure against her breasts. His lips were parted, fanning her mouth with his breath, his eyes were alive with smoldering embers, filling the whole world with their electric hypnotic light.

He lifted his hands to cup her face, and his kiss was so close she could taste it. Her eyes started to drift close as his face drew nearer to hers. And then he stopped. She could feel his deep, calming breath. He said, somewhat huskily, "Allison, you've got to give me your answer pretty soon."

She opened her eyes, making herself focus on him, grinding down frustration. "Why?"

His thumbs caressed the corners of her mouth. "Because I don't know how much longer I can keep from kissing you."

His thumb slipped inside her parted lips, just a fraction, and she tasted his skin with the tip of her tongue. Her throat convulsed. It was a moment before she could say anything at all. "Why can't you kiss me before I give you my answer?"

He smiled, gently and regretfully, and let his hands fall away. "I don't want to be accused of using undue influence."

"A kiss," she said, holding his gaze, "is just a kiss."

A spark of passion caught and flared deep within his eyes, and the sight of it was enough to take Allison's breath away. But almost as quickly as it had surged it was brought under control, and his smile deepened. A world of promise lived in that smile.

"So it is," he agreed, and moved away.

He took her hand and led her carefully down the last few steps. By the time they reached the bottom her heartbeat was almost normal and her breathing under control. The intensity of the episode on the stairs began to fade and Stone's voice, when he spoke, was very close to casual.

"So there you have it—the grand tour, reserved for very important people whom I want to impress very badly." He led her forward into the famous banquet room where—in Modesto, at least—the lord of the manor was murdered by his lady in a particularly gruesome fashion and where, one was given to assume, the dinner guests would play an important role in concealing the evidence of the crime.

"Generally we end the tour with a banquet served here," Stone added, gesturing toward the long oak table that was set, as was its counterpart in Modesto, with ornate goblets and silver plates, awaiting the unsuspecting diners. "Sorry I didn't know you were coming."

Allison slanted him a warning look. "I don't even want to ask what's on the menu."

Stone chuckled and hoisted himself onto the corner of the table with barely a rattle of tableware, resting one foot on the low trestle bench beside him. "So," he said invitingly with an expansive gesture. "What do you think?"

Allison looked around, as awed by the rough stone walls, the age-worn tapestries, the walk-in fireplace and scarred wooden candelabra as she had been when she had first seen it in Yesteryear Park. "I'm impressed," she said. "And honored to be included among the elite. But what woman wouldn't be?"

"Actually," he admitted with a small frown, as though the fact surprised him, "I've never brought a woman down here before—except in a professional capacity, of course."

They both seemed to realize what he had said at once. If he didn't regard Allison in a professional capacity, how did he see her? And if he had not brought her here as part of his sales pitch, why had he shared with her something that was obviously so important to him, something he had just admitted he did not do for everyone?

Stone did not seem to have an answer any more than Allison did, and his next statement only further confused her—and, from the deepening shadow of disturbance in his eyes, himself as well. "As a matter of fact, you're the first person outside the company to ever see the Celiton Three program I ran at the beginning. It's the showpiece of the Heroshito project, and I was going to unveil it next month."

A thrill went through her, both with the knowledge that she had shared something with him only a privileged few had ever known before, and with the remembrance of the wonder she had experienced—both from the illusion, and being in his arms. "It was incredible," she said sincerely.

The smile that filled his eyes was rich with understanding and appreciation. He extended his hands to her and, without ever having intended to take the first step, she walked to him. He caught her hands and drew her gently between his knees. His eyes were like silver, and there was a glint of gold in the stubble on his cheeks. He said quietly, "I want you to know that even if this hadn't come up, I was already trying to think of ways to see you again."

His hands were warm and his grip firm but gentle. Her pulse speeded of its own accord. She believed him. She knew she was a fool for doing so, but she did. "I thought you weren't going to use undue influence."

He smiled. Her heart melted. "I'm trying not to."

She made a somewhat feeble effort to tug her hands away. Although a good three inches of table separated her thigh from his pelvis, she imagined she could feel his heat radiating through her clothing. "It's not always a good idea to mix business and pleasure. Particularly this kind of business."

"Does that mean you'll help me?"

She made herself pull her hands free. He let her go. She had to turn away from him, giving her head a chance to clear. She steepled her fingers and after a moment she said, "Let me get this straight. You want me to lie to perfect strangers—"

"I prefer to think of it as pretending."

"You want me to lie," she repeated firmly, "just so that you can get a job for which one of the requirements is the very thing you're lying about?"

Stone looked briefly confused and Allison couldn't blame him. She wasn't entirely sure she understood what she had said herself. Then he said dismissively, "It's a stupid rule, arbitrary and discriminatory and you know it as well as I do. If it were something important—or even relevant—it would be different. But I've all but won the contract on my talent alone, which is the way it should be. The only thing that stands in my way is some random personal preference that has nothing to do with my qualifications for the job and they *deserve* to be deceived about that."

Allison had no argument for that. She never had.

"Come on," he said persuasively. "Didn't you ever play make believe as a kid? That's all it is, just another game of make believe and you've got to admit we were damn good at it last night."

Allison looked at him, long and studiously. She said. "I have a feeling there's too much make believe in your life as it is." She made a sweeping gesture around the room. "All of this—you're just a big kid living in a toy shop. You don't have the faintest idea what the real world is about."

A relaxed twinkle came into his eyes. "The perfect life," he agreed.

A challenge, his mother had said. An opportunity no one before her had ever been offered...that was an understatement.

She said abruptly, "I'll do it." And she raised a hand to forestall the enthusiastic response she could see forming. "But I want you to know it's purely a business decision. We need the contacts you've given us and we don't want to lose your goodwill. That's all."

The twinkle did not fade. "That's all? Not because you like me, even a little?"

She said firmly, "No."

"Liar."

"That's beside the point."

He laughed and jumped down from the table, coming toward her. "We're going to have fun, Allison," he declared, catching her hands. "And if I had to get caught in a lie I couldn't have picked a better person to do it with. Thank you," he added seriously. "You won't be sorry."

But when she lifted her eyes to his and felt his warmth start to melt through her again, she was already sorry. She was helpless in his hands. And she was sure she had just made the biggest mistake of her life.

Even as she watched, his eyes kindled again with that inner spark, his gaze moved over her face, her lips, her breasts and back again to her eyes. He said, "As for not mixing business with pleasure...I'll try. But no promises."

Allison was glad. She nodded, and her voice was a little thick as she responded, "Fair enough."

"Done." He smiled. "Shall we seal it with a kiss?"

Allison tugged her fingers from his and deliberately offered her hand to shake. "Business," she reminded him firmly.

He laughed. "We *are* going to have fun!"

He flung an arm around her shoulders in a companionable gesture and turned to lead her from the room. "So," he continued conversationally, "how soon can you move in?"

Eight

Allison did not move in, but Stone had not expected it to be that easy. She did, however, accept responsibility for starting the rumor that swept through the circle of Stone's friends and acquaintances within twelve hours, and she came up with an ingenious solution to what could have been a sticky situation. She helped him record a new message for his home answering machine: "Hello, this is Stone—and Allison—we're sorry we can't come to the phone right now..." and sent over a small box of toiletries for the sake of his housekeeper—a worn toothbrush, some old makeup she was getting ready to throw away, a half-empty box of dusting powder. Stone felt a little odd about displaying these things on his bathroom counter at first, but soon discovered he rather liked the way they looked. The dusting powder in particular. He had accidentally knocked the container over one morning while shaving and the bathroom had smelled like her the rest of the day.

She even brought over a few dresses that she said were on their way to Goodwill and hung them in his closet. He liked the way that looked, too. And as a final touch, she supplied a framed picture of herself for his office desk, though Stone had to take credit for that idea. He had noticed similar photographs on the desks of his married friends and detail, as he knew very well, was the key to authenticity.

What he had never understood before was *why* men kept photographs of their wives or lovers on their desks, and he had been giving the question considerable thought over the past ten days or so since Allison came into his life. He liked looking at the photograph, of course. In it she was wearing a cable-knit sweater, her hair was wind-tossed and her cheeks flushed and her eyes sparkling. The ocean was in the background and she was laughing. It was a great photograph and he never tired of looking at it. But he was beginning to suspect there was something more than aesthetic value to the entire ritual of women's photos on men's desks. He looked at that picture a dozen times a day and every time he discovered something new. But the main thing he discovered was a sense of connection, a reminder that outside the office someone waited, outside the world he created was another world, another life, and it was an odd feeling. It was something he had never really thought about before. Days would pass without his even talking to her. He hadn't seen her for more than a few minutes at a time since he had brought her here for the grand tour, and yet she was never out of his mind, never far apart from him. He looked at her picture and he felt a sense of belonging, of being part of a couple, and even though he knew it was only make believe, that was a feeling he thought he could grow to like very easily.

He was looking at the photograph for the last time that day when Carla pushed open his door and came inside. She stopped and looked around the office in astonishment. The desk was cleared, the computer down, the drafting board and electronics safely locked behind their glass-front cabinets, his day's work filed away.

"My God," said Carla. "The woman is not only a saint, but she's a miracle worker. You haven't been ready to go home this early since I came to work for you."

Carla knew the truth about his *engagement,* for he could no more deceive her than he could his mother. As had his mother, she heartily disapproved at first, but had undergone a steady transformation of opinion in the last week or so since Allison had begun to actively organize his life.

He put the photograph back on the desk and picked up his jacket from the chair on which he had tossed it that morning. "We're giving our first dinner party," he told Carla with a wink. "And I get the feeling that if I'm late I won't want to live to tell the tale."

"Like this would be the first dinner party you'd ever been late for? What kind of magic has this lady got?"

Stone hooked his finger through the collar tab of his jacket and slung it over one shoulder. "You don't need magic," he assured Carla, grinning, "when a multimillion-dollar contract is hanging in the balance."

"Ah, so that's all it takes to teach you manners. And I always thought you were impervious to bribes."

He gave her face a friendly pat on the way out. "You just haven't found my price yet."

But she was right. When Stone was in the middle of a project, he never left the office before 10:00 p.m. and sometimes stayed through the night, napping on the sofa between manic bouts of inspiration. And even he was self-aware enough to wonder just how much of his eagerness to get home was due to the contract that could very well be at stake, and how much of it was simply because he knew Allison would be there.

Stone had a condo on the north side of town that was high-security, high-prestige and decorator appointed. He had lived there for four years and if asked could not have fully described even one of its six rooms. When he dined it was usually out or with friends, and for the most part the only time he used the condo was to change clothes, or occasionally, to sleep. That was why, when Mark's wife, Sarah, had called to invite him and Allison to dinner, Stone had considered it a stroke of genius to invite them to his place instead. Entertaining at home was something a family man did, and authenticity of detail was of paramount importance to the success of his scheme.

He didn't entirely understand why Allison did not share his enthusiasm for the dinner party, but he knew that it had something to do with the fact that he had only told her about it that morning. Remembering the icy silence that had greeted his announcement of his plans over the phone was only one of the reasons he had determined to be home in plenty of time to help.

When he walked into the condo he almost didn't recognize the place, and it was plain to see his help was the last thing that was needed. Everything gleamed and sparkled with a subtle elegance. A vase of fresh flowers graced the low Oriental table in the foyer. More flowers decorated the cocktail table in the living room and formed the centerpiece of the long black lacquer dining table. A fire burned in the grate—he could not recall ever having used the fireplace before—and classical music was playing softly on the stereo. The table was set with black dinnerware on bright yellow placemats, with yellow-and-red napkins rolled up in the wineglasses. Something exquisite was baking in the kitchen and, for a moment, all Stone wanted to do was just stand there and inhale the fragrance.

He called, "Allison?"

He moved through the room, pausing to touch the flowers, to examine the stemware, to admire the platter of artfully arranged hors d'oeuvre on the cocktail table and to approve the bar. He started to pour himself a drink—a luxury he had never enjoyed in his own home before for the simple reason that he never remembered to stock the bar—then changed his mind. The best part about the entire arrangement was that tonight he didn't have to drink alone.

He called again, "Allison!" and when he got no reply he started up the stairs.

He met her coming out of the guest room. She was wearing a red dress with a scooped neck and long, tight sleeves, a body-hugging torso that flared into a full graceful calf-length skirt. From the curve of her breasts to the slender line of her waist to the gentle flare of her hips; from her tousled hair to her white shoulders to the feminine curve of her collarbone to the faint, tantalizing hint of décolletage; from the depths of her startled blue eyes to the tips of her stockinged feet, she was enough to stop any man in his tracks.

She had a hairbrush in her hand, and one of her sleeves was unbuttoned. For no discernible reason the surprise in her eyes turned to annoyance and she said, "You're early."

He tried to keep his eyes from straying to the deliciously defined, elegantly adorned shape of her breasts. "I thought I'd help."

"*Now* you offer! Thanks, but I've got things under control." She gestured behind her. "I used your guest bath to shower and change. I hope you don't mind."

"Of course not. The place looks great. If I had known coming home could be like this I would have done it more often."

That brought a small, reluctant smile to her lips and she turned to go back into the guest room. "That's my job, you know. I cook, I decorate, I organize. I prefer, however..." She tossed him a scathing look over his shoulder. "To do it with slightly more than six hours notice."

"Be sure to send me a bill." He followed her inside the guest room and leaned against the door. The smell of steamy soap and dusting powder brought a small, pleasured smile to his lips.

"You'd better believe it. Honestly, Stone..." She bent at the waist and brushed her hair vigorously from the underside. "It's no wonder you can't keep a girlfriend for more than a month at a time. Did you have to practice being this inconsiderate or is it something that comes naturally?"

"Just lucky, I guess."

She straightened up, her hair floating around her face in an artful swirl, and glared at him. "You really *are* incorrigible, aren't you?"

He pushed away from the door frame, smiling easily. "Let me button your sleeve for you."

"Well," she admitted grudgingly, "you did get here on time. I guess that's some kind of progress."

She extended her arm to him and he began to work the small looped buttons that ran the underside of her wrist. Her perfume was like a sweet warm intoxicant when he stood that close, and he could see the gentle rise and fall of her breasts with each breath. He had never imagined before that fastening buttons could be just as erotic as unfastening them. It took all his willpower to keep from showing just how stimulating he found the process to be.

But the moment the last button was nestled inside its loop she pulled her arm away and turned back to the mirror. "You've got about forty-five minutes to change," she said.

She took a hair clasp from a small flowered bag on the dresser and swept her hair up on top of her head, pinning it deftly. Her cheeks seemed a little flushed and Stone felt a catch of excitement in his chest when he noticed, wondering if the color was in reaction to him. He wanted to find out. He wanted to move close behind her, to rest his hands on her waist, to drop a kiss on the smooth white curve of her neck that her upswept hair exposed. But some dim and rarely exercised instinct—something that had to do with gentlemanly behavior—warned him that such a move would not be wise at that moment. And the impression was only reinforced by the wary way in which she watched him in the mirror as she donned a pair of gold loop earrings.

So he merely grinned, and turned toward the door. "It's nice to have a woman in the house," he told her, and he meant it.

The moment he was gone Allison released a long, pent-up breath and leaned back against the dresser, letting her muscles go limp. She was as nervous as a new bride at her first sit-down dinner, and to have Stone come home so unexpectedly, to look up and see him standing there, lean and sexy and perfectly at ease in his own home while she met him, still damp from the shower, in bare feet and disarranged hair... It was disconcerting to say the least. It was hard to remember that she was only doing a job.

The truth was, she had prepared bigger dinners on shorter notice and the afternoon she had spent in an unfamiliar kitchen was no hardship on her. She had prepared the recipes a hundred times, the florist and cleaning service were as efficient as ever, the table setting and centerpiece were practically industry standard. She could have pulled this one off in her sleep... except for one thing.

That one thing was Stone. While she worked in his kitchen she wondered if he ever cooked there. When she touched a match to the logs in the fireplace she imagined him sitting before it on long, lonely nights, staring into the flames. She wondered who had decorated his apartment, who had picked out his dinnerware, and she spent more time than she should have perusing his record collection, making a selection for dinner. Worst of all, the dishes she prepared were chosen because she thought he would like them, not because a well-planned meal was part of her job. The dress she wore was chosen specifically with him in mind, and not because looking good was part of the role she had agreed to play in order to impress Stone's business associates. She wanted to inspire in his eyes the very spark she had seen when he looked at her.

Over the past ten days she had been very careful to conduct the majority of their business over the phone, to keep their meetings brief and businesslike, to allow herself no opportunity to be alone with him in anything that might remotely be construed as a personal situation. The reason? He was very nearly irresistible, and she knew that very well. Her only hope was to keep their relationship as distant and professional as possible. Yet the moment she walked into his apartment it didn't feel as if it was business anymore. She cooked his meal, she set his table, she stepped into his shower and she wasn't just doing a job—she was a part of his life.

No one had to tell her that an attitude such as that could be very dangerous to a woman who had not entered into a contract to have her heart broken. But it had been an awfully long time since Allison had lived dangerously.

He came into the kitchen just as she was taking the broccoli casserole from the oven. "Which one?" he said.

She placed the casserole on the cooling rack and turned, removing the oven mitts. He was freshly shaved and showered, his hair still a little damp at the temples. He was wearing pleated gray wool slacks and a beautifully tailored shirt in a shade of pale pink that very few men could carry off. In either hand he held a tie—one in a classic pink-and-gray stripe, the other gray-on-black. The scene was so cozily domestic that Allison had to grin.

"That one," she said, choosing the pink and gray. "It's an informal evening, after all."

"Gee, I never can remember that rule."

"But," she added severely, "don't you dare ask me to tie it for you—that's just too, too cute."

He grinned as he tossed the discarded tie over the back of a chair at the breakfast nook and threaded the other one beneath his collar. "Something smells great in here."

"Chicken Dijon, garden salad, broccoli casserole and strawberry shortcake with coffee."

"God, real food. I always figured I'd marry a woman who cooked real food—or at least ate it. This is the first meal I've had in months that didn't have the word mousse or poached in it."

Allison laughed as she opened the refrigerator door. "Well, I could have served steak and potatoes, but I thought that might be too obvious. You have a great kitchen."

"Do I? I never use it."

She began to transfer the salad from the serving bowl to individual salad bowls, carefully placing the garnishes atop each while Stone used the reflective surface of the toaster oven to place the knot in his tie. "I'd forgotten how nice a kitchen could be," he admitted. "Maybe I'll start eating here sometimes."

"I can't believe no one has ever made you dinner in your own kitchen before."

"Actually no one has. I just never thought to ask, I guess, and the relationships never last long enough for her to suggest it."

Allison glanced at him askance. "There's really something a little pathological about a man who can't even maintain a relationship long enough to have a woman over for dinner."

"Short attention span," he admitted, straightening up with a very close-to-perfect Windsor knot in his tie. "Six weeks, max. Is there something manly I can do around here? I'm no good with vegetable peelers or cheese graters."

Allison grinned and nodded toward the wine on the counter. "How about opening that bottle? Is that manly enough for you?"

"Naturally I'd feel better if it were a beer can. A guy who suffered through four years of ballroom dancing has a right to be sensitive about these things, you know."

Allison laughed softly. He had promised her fun, and he hadn't lied.

"We need to decide on our story," Allison reminded him as she began to return the salads to the refrigerator. "Your friends are bound to ask questions and we have to make sure our answers match. The first thing is how and when we met. We already told that car-bumper thing to your friend Carolyn, and I guess we could elaborate on that..."

"Why not the truth?" Stone suggested.

She paused, half in and half out of the refrigerator, and rolled her eyes at him. "Now why do you suppose I didn't think of that?" she murmured.

"No, I mean it." He twisted the corkscrew. "Or at least stay as close to the truth as possible. It's easier to remember that way."

"Coming from a man who deals in deception . . ."

"And knows the easiest way to fool the eye is to stick as closely to what people *expect* to see as possible. Same principle." The cork came free with a small pop, and he set the bottle on the counter. "You came to my office to talk about doing that dinner party for the Heroshito people next month..."

Allison shook her head, closing the refrigerator door. "Won't work. The timing is off. You would have had to have met me and asked me to marry you in the same day."

"Love at first sight," he suggested.

"No one will believe that."

"Of course they will."

She was sponging off the counter and her back was to him. She did not see him come toward her until his hands were on her waist, turning her gently to face him. Even then she hadn't expected him to be so close. He filled her entire vision—he filled, in fact, every sense. That wild forest scent of his suffused her, his warmth crept into her skin like a slow immersion in a hot spring. Her backside was pressed against the counter. His thighs and his pelvis trapped her gently, with no pressure at all, against him while his hands, leaving her waist, drifted lightly down the shape of her arms, brushing them with a touch. His eyes, smoky and luminous with a low, sensual light, filled the world.

"It happened like this," he said softly. "You came to my office. The minute I saw you I knew there was something special about you. Maybe it was that short little skirt you were wearing, or the black stockings." He smiled. "I've always been a pushover for black stockings."

Allison smiled, too, trying to bring her heartbeat back under control, and started to turn away. But he wasn't finished.

His hands drifted up her arms, cupping the shape of her shoulders, tracing with the barest of feathery touches the shape of her collarbone and her throat. With that touch, with his gaze, he held Allison hypnotized.

"Maybe," he said, moving his hand upward, tracing the shape of her hair without touching it, "it was the way you wore your hair pulled back from your face with that band, like a little girl, but not innocent. Maybe it was the way you moved or the way you spoke, or the way your eyes flashed when you got mad... but everything about you went right through me, like someone threw a spear right into my soul. It stopped me cold. I never thought it would happen to me but it did, right there in my office in a matter of minutes. I was smitten. You walked in and I had to have you and I knew from that minute on, as clearly as I've ever known anything, that my life would never be the same."

Only make believe, Allison told herself. *That's all it is, a fantasy he's spinning, a tale to tell...* But he was so very good at it. Her throat was dry and she had to part her lips for breath and she felt herself being drawn into the depths of those dream-making eyes, in danger of being lost forever.

The backs of his knuckles caressed her cheek, and his gaze followed the movement. "And you," he said huskily. "You looked at me and you saw it. You felt it, too—something magic, something special, something you knew you couldn't let get away. We kissed."

Slowly he dropped his lips to hers, pressing a light, tender, exquisitely sensual kiss on her mouth. Brief though it was, fever surged, chemicals inside her body exploded in a reckless riot. When he lifted his face, she raised her arms as though to draw him back to her but then, with a great force of will, she stopped, resting her hands against his chest.

His eyes burned with a slow consuming fire as they moved slowly over her face, and everywhere his gaze touched was like a brand. His breath fanned her parted lips, and his voice was low and husky. "I took you to my castle," he said. Lowering his face, he placed a slow, heated kiss at the juncture of her collarbone. "We made love in the queen's bedchamber." Another kiss, just beneath her earlobe. Allison's knees lost their rigidity. "You set my soul on fire, you crawled inside my skin, you were the beginning and the end of everything I had ever known. Together..." His fingertips slid inside the material that covered her shoulder, moving it aside a fraction of an inch. He tasted the skin he had exposed with his tongue. "We were magic."

Allison lost her breath, her head spun and none of it was pretend anymore. She whispered, "Stone..."

His hand cupped her neck, and when he placed another kiss, long and hard and hot, in the hollow of her throat, her head fell back helplessly, arching into it. "We couldn't see the future without each other in it. I asked you to marry me. You said yes. We've never regretted it, not for a minute."

His voice was throaty and his breath was not quite even. His heat flared through her and she could feel his heartbeat, quick and strong, against her hand. If he kissed her, just once, there would be no turning back, no more pretending, and nothing would make sense ever again. And even though every instinct in her body cried out to draw him closer, she stiffened her hands, pushing slightly against his chest. She said hoarsely, "Stone, please . . ."

For a moment he seemed not to have heard her. The light in his eyes was enough to set her skin aflame, and he lifted his hands as though to thrust them through her hair, to pull her to him and cover her mouth with his, drinking of her. And though she wanted it fiercely, savagely, he must have read a more desperate signal in her eyes, because he stopped. His hands hovered in the air beside her head for a moment as though with a final, unseen caress, and then he dropped them, in a deliberately casual motion, to her shoulders.

He lowered his eyes briefly. When he looked at her again the fire was almost, but not entirely, under control. He said, "It could happen."

Allison swallowed hard, but it was another moment before she could speak. Even then her voice was thick and hoarse. "Two weeks," she said. "We'd known each other two weeks."

"One day. Otherwise I would've still been dating Susan and everyone knows I'm strictly monogamous."

"Nobody will believe this."

"It could happen," he insisted.

And the disturbing thing was, Allison was beginning to believe it could.

The doorbell rang, and they separated with a startled, guilty abruptness.

"My God, can that be them already?" Allison's hands flew to her hot cheeks, her hair, and she brushed at the folds of her skirt. "Look at me, I'm a mess! Is my lipstick smudged?"

Stone grinned. "Relax, you look exactly like any soon-to-be bride is supposed to look." And then he snapped his fingers with sudden remembrance. "Speaking of which—" he reached into his pocket "—I picked you up a little something today."

Between his thumb and forefinger he held a diamond solitaire.

Allison gasped. "Stone! I-it's not real, is it?"

"Of course not." He reached for her hand. "But the man at the store said only an expert could tell the difference." He slipped the ring onto the third finger of her left hand. "What do you think?"

Allison spread her fingers, admiring the glitter of the stone in the light and feeling a little thrill of awe that was as old as the nature of womanhood itself. The setting was unquestionably gold, even she knew that much. The zircon was round-cut, about two carats and mounted on either side with two small stones that were either emeralds or very good imitations. He said it wasn't a diamond and she believed him, but that in no way mitigated the beauty of the ring, or the thrill of seeing it on her finger.

She asked, "How did you know my size?"

"I asked your partner."

She lowered her hand, smiling at him. "You remembered that an engagement calls for a ring? You called my partner to find out my size? You went all the way to the jewelers to pick it out yourself? Stone Harrison..." She slipped her arm through his, leading him toward the door. "There may be hope for you yet."

Dinner was an unqualified success. And more than dinner—the entire evening practically glowed. Mark and Sarah Farmington were easy to like. Even though it was obvious they were grilling Stone and interviewing Allison, they did it in such a relaxed, good-humored way it was impossible to resent them for it. And, as amazing as it was, Allison and Stone passed every test. When Stone began his absurd story about their whirlwind courtship, Allison found herself falling in step, embellishing details in such a natural way that not a single eyebrow was raised in question or disbelief. A tender touch here, a loving look there, a shared smile across the room—even Allison found it easy to believe that the two of them were deep in the throes of a long and lasting passion. And as the evening progressed she noticed that she was reminding herself less and less often to pretend.

There was only one awkward moment, and that was when Sarah asked innocently whether they had set the date. Stone replied, without hesitation, "November 16." And reached for Allison's hand.

Allison foresaw immediately the problems such a concrete detail would cause, and she looked at Stone in alarm. But he merely smiled and brought her fingers to his lips and Allison couldn't have voiced an objection even if she wanted to. Sarah immediately began to exclaim over the shortness of the time—the wedding date was less than two months away—and Allison fielded questions about the ceremony and the reception and china patterns. If it hadn't been for the wonderfully soothing, subtly erotic motions Stone's thumb was making over her wrist she probably would have kicked him in the shins.

At eleven o'clock that night they sat together on the sofa, sipping brandy, basking in the glow of the fire and the radiance of success. Their feet were propped up side by side on the coffee table, Stone's arm was stretched over the back of the sofa and Allison rested her head on his shoulder. Such was the conviction of the roles they had played all evening that it seemed only natural.

"We were magnificent," Stone decided in a tone rich with satisfaction.

Allison nodded, smiling drowsily into her brandy. Exhaustion, triumph, the simple exhilaration of Stone's presence and perhaps even the brandy had combined to leave her slightly soporific, floating on air. "I've got to give you credit," she admitted, "I never thought we could pull it off. But they didn't have the first shadow of a suspicion. They left here thinking we were a match made in heaven."

Stone's fingers moved absently over her hair, making a pattern of tucking strands behind her ear. She could feel his eyes on her, and the smile that caressed her just as tenderly as his fingers did. "I told you," he said. "We're perfect together."

She looked up at him, mostly to move her head away from the delicious, tantalizing motions of his fingers. "Whatever possessed you to give them a date? That's going to backfire on us, you know. What's going to happen when November 16 comes and there's no wedding?"

"The contract has to be awarded by October thirtieth. On October 31 we have a fight, the wedding's off and no one's the wiser."

"That's cutting it awfully close," she said, worried.

"Maybe. But I figured a long engagement would be out of character for two people as much in love as we are."

Again she looked up at him, startled, and a split second later realized he was referring to the roles they played, not to the reality. She hid her confusion with another sip of brandy.

"Dinner was great, by the way," Stone added after a moment. It seemed to Allison that he, too, was a little self-conscious about the previous slip and was searching for a neutral subject. "Everything was. Do you really like doing all that—cooking and arranging flowers and rolling up napkins into wineglasses? Most women I know would think that was beneath their dignity."

Allison laughed a little, relaxing. "Most women I know, too. But I really like it. I wanted to be a *Cordon Bleu* chef once—almost got to study in Paris. And even as a kid I threw the best doll tea parties in town."

He sipped his brandy. "What happened to Paris?"

She shrugged. "By that time I'd found something else I wanted more." And she slanted a glance at him. "Short attention span."

His eyes danced and his hand cupped the back of Allison's neck in a friendly, companionable manner. "See? We *do* have a lot in common."

"I grew out of it," she said deliberately.

"Then, as you said, maybe there's hope for me." He tasted the brandy again. "Is that your dream then? Paris, the *Cordon Bleu?*"

She laughed softly. "Goodness, no. What would make you ask a thing like that?"

"Fantasy is my business," he reminded her. His voice was casual, his manner relaxed. His fingertips began to knead the back of her neck in a slow, rhythmic fashion that sent languorous ripples of warmth down her spine. "Everyone has a dream. What's yours?"

Maybe it was the brandy, the lazily dancing patterns of the low-burning fire, the slow sensual movements of his fingers along the back of her neck, but she murmured, "This."

She could feel his surprise, and the brief, almost imperceptible pause in the motion of his fingers. She smiled and glanced up at him, then back into her brandy glass. "I mean . . ." She made a vague gesture with her left hand, and the ring flashed in the firelight. "All of it. The diamond ring, the elegant dinner for four, the brandy and firelight . . . the engagement parties, the rehearsal dinner, the ivory satin and white roses. That's my fantasy." And she turned her face to look up at him, feeling a little shy. "I suppose I should thank you for giving me a chance to live it out."

His eyes were rich and dark, his smile gentle. "My pleasure," he said softly.

His fingers left her neck and caressed the shape of her ear, teasing her jawline, stroking her cheek. A shiver of awareness went through her when his fingertip outlined her parted lips. His eyes, quiet and steady and alive with pleasure, signaled his intent, and she could have stopped him if she had wanted. Instead, when his mouth covered hers she lifted her face to drink him in, she let him flood her with heat and dizziness, she tasted him in every pore of her being. Her arm crept up to encircle his neck and she spread her fingers through the silky luxury of his hair. She heard the warning bells, she knew it was dangerous, but the allure of the fantasy was powerful and his seduction expert. She let herself savor it, knowing that common sense would reassert itself all too soon. It always did.

When his lips left hers, she was aching and dizzy. She could feel the quick tempo of his breath across her face. He took the glass of brandy from her numbed fingers, and when he returned to her she managed to avert her face only a fraction. "Stone," she whispered. "Please..."

"What?" His lips brushed across hers with the word. His hand moved in a slow, sensuous caress down her side, from the curve of her upraised arm to her hip. The fingers of his other hand were strong against the back of her neck, supporting her weight.

It was with a very great effort that Allison steadied her voice, made herself look straight into his eyes. "It's just make believe, remember?" she said. "Don't get carried away with your role."

He smiled. That smile went through her with the same devastating effect his caress had done, melting her emotions the way his touch had melted her body. "Is that what I'm doing?"

"I—think so." But her words lacked conviction, because the gentle brush of his lips closed her eyes. His hand skimmed across her waist, making feather-light circling motions across her abdomen. All she had to do was catch his hand, stop the caress. But she didn't.

"Is that what you're doing?" His tongue traced the shape of her lips, heat and moisture, salt and brandy. She tasted him. She savored him.

"I—yes. No. I don't know."

And then both hands came up to cup her face, and he was silent for so long that she had to open her eyes. His gaze was intent, his expression sober. He said quietly, "Does it matter?"

And that was her chance—to back away, to play it safe, to retreat back into the world of reality where she belonged. But it was no longer so easy to remember where reality began and fantasy ended. That day she had walked into his office had it been love at first sight or a case of mistaken identity? That night they had danced into the morning had the delight they discovered in each other's arms been imagination? And when he kissed her had he been only pretending? Hadn't she known even then that everything between them, whether real or make believe, was only leading them to this moment?

It should have mattered. And if she said that it did, he would not push. The line would be drawn and neither of them would ever stray across it again.

She whispered, "No." And she drew him down to her again.

He carried her upstairs. In her most romantic fantasies she had always pictured being swept off her feet, carried up a long, sweeping staircase, being laid gently upon a canopy-draped bed. The staircase was not very long or sweeping but she was definitely swept off her feet. The movement from sofa to bed was a blur of breaths and heartbeats and when they reached the bed, she was hardly aware of the surface beneath her because already his hands, his lips, had begun to work their sense-stripping magic.

He divested her of her garments with exquisite slowness and tender care, prolonging the pleasure to its most agonizing point, making her want to cry out with need even before the first layer was removed. Each button on her sleeve was released from its loop, and the skin thus exposed was caressed by his tongue. The long zipper down the back of her dress was parted slowly, exposing her spine to the cool room temperature and the warmth of his lips. He pushed the material of her dress off her shoulders, drawing his tongue in lazy circular patterns over her chest, pressing heat and moisture into the sheer fabric of her bra, moving lower, across her rib cage and to her abdomen, where he slipped his fingers beneath the waistband of her panty hose and drew them downward with the material of her dress.

He slipped his hand beneath the back of her knee, drawing her leg upward, and she gasped out loud with the sensation of his tongue lightly tracing the inside of her thigh. The wire of longing that stretched from her breasts to her abdomen tightened sharply and spread to a heavy aching between her thighs and she thought dizzily, *I should have known. I should have known with him it would be like this*...

Somehow her impatient hands had tugged open the buttons of his shirt and when he stretched above her she felt the brief hot pressure of his naked chest against her breasts, she felt the smooth, strong length of his back beneath her exploring hands. His kiss enveloped her, leaving her dizzy. He unfastened the clasp of her bra and his mouth moved to cover her breasts. Waves of pleasure spun through her as his slow, drawing kisses penetrated her most sensitive flesh. His hand caressed her hip and moved with a delicate, feather-light touch over the inside of her thigh, caressing her through the silky fabric of her panties and then, slowly slipping inside...

Making love with Stone was like wading into an ocean of pleasure, being submerged by wave after wave, each one more intense, more consuming. She was swept away by the delight he offered, caught in a web of rapture, helpless to resist his enchantment. She hardly knew when the last of his clothes were discarded, when her wondering hands at last explored the full-length of his strength and nakedness. His heat infused her, his breath became her own, his eyes the only blur of light in the darkness. She felt his thighs gently separating hers, the sweet, low pressure of his entry, filling her, becoming part of her. She kissed his mouth, she memorized his face with her hands, she gave herself over to the expanding spirals of pleasure he created within her and she thought dizzily, *It could happen. The magic, the wonder, the miracle...it could happen.* And she knew then that he was more than just a fantasy—he was every dream she had ever had come true.

Afterward they lay together in stunned recognition of the wonder they had shared, holding each other while the world slowly righted itself. His fingers caressed her shoulder and his lips pressed against her hair. Allison smiled to herself, secretly and sadly, because she knew what he was thinking. Magic was a part of his life. Tonight he had brought that magic to her and his greatest pleasure was in doing so, but both of them had known from the beginning it wasn't meant to last.

She could not expect more from him than he was willing to give. That had not been part of their bargain.

She lay against the beat of his heart and she understood why women loved him, knowing they could not claim him. She understood why they accepted what he offered knowing that one of the terms of his affection was that it could not last. No one had the right to try to possess him, Allison least of all. The only promise he had ever made her was that they would have fun.

Yet she felt the tenderness in his touch, the concern in his voice as he said, "Allison, I don't want you to..."

She turned over, resting her head on his shoulder and threading her fingers through his. "I just didn't have the courage," she said thoughtfully.

The caressing motions of his hand against her arm stopped. "What?"

She brought their entwined fingers to her face, stroking her cheek with his knuckles. "Paris," she said. "A crazy artist who wanted me to live with him on love and promises. Hitchhiking to New Orleans, even moving to Canada... every adventure I've almost ever had I've backed away from at the last minute because I just didn't have the courage to take a chance and let go... to do something just for the fun of it."

She turned over then, propping herself up on one elbow, sliding her knee between his legs. Her eyes sparkled as she looked down at him. "You're the biggest adventure I've ever had, Stone Harrison," she said. "And I'm already having more fun than I've ever had in my life."

And as he drew her down into his embrace she believed that was enough. She truly did.

Nine

Penny said worriedly, "I really don't like this. I mean, it looks to me like you're starting to get carried away by the whole thing."

"Oh, for heaven's sake." Allison stood in front of the foyer mirror, holding first a blue scarf, then a rust-colored one next to the lapel of the camel-colored suit she was wearing. "It's just lunch with some of Stone's friends."

"What kind of man has that many women friends? And why do they want to take you to lunch?"

"You never heard of a bridal luncheon?"

Allison met Penny's eyes in the mirror and felt her cheeks warm. She quickly shifted her gaze away. "What I mean is, that's part of the job. I agreed to pretend to be Stone's fiancée—"

"To help him get a contract," Penny pointed out. "Going to lunch with the girls doesn't have a thing to do with impressing his business associates and..." She drew in a breath. "I'd be willing to bet Stone doesn't even know you're going."

"Of course he knows," Allison replied irritably, tossing aside the rust-colored scarf. "His own mother's going to be there." She looped the blue scarf around her neck, knotted it, then jerked it off. It looked awful. "I don't know what difference it makes to you anyway. You were the one who thought the whole thing was such a great idea when it first came up."

"I only thought going out with him was a great idea," Penny said, correcting her. "But if it makes you feel better to blame me for this whole getting-engaged fiasco go ahead. It's just that—Allison, I'm worried about you. I mean, this whole thing started out as a joke and now... well, look at you. You've practically moved in with him. You don't have time for any other clients and just when we've finally got work..." When Allison opened her mouth to protest she overrode her. "No, that's okay. That's not even the point. It's just that..." Her expression was tentative, apologetic. "The man made it perfectly clear this is only a temporary arrangement, but you just seem to be getting more and more wrapped up in it and I wonder sometimes if you're starting to forget that ring on your finger is only a zircon."

Allison endured what felt to her to be an unjustified tirade of accusations stalwartly, deliberately arranging the rust-colored scarf across one shoulder of her suit. But not very far below the surface she recognized the truth in every word Penny spoke, and it hurt.

She had not told Penny that she and Stone were lovers, but she suspected her friend knew. She *had* almost moved in with Stone. Every night was spent with him, if not at his home then at his office, and though she justified the time—to herself and others—as necessary for the final spectacular dinner party she planned for the Heroshito group, the time she spent with Stone could not by any stretch of the imagination be considered part of the job. Certainly they worked on the evening of spectacle, entertainment and presentation Allison had designed and it was an exciting, fulfilling task, but when the work ended—and if they didn't make love—they stayed together, talking, laughing, being easy together.... Sooner or later they made love, because doing so was as natural as breathing and because the chemistry that drew them together never seemed to fade no matter how close they became. When she was with Stone everything seemed so simple, so easy to understand, so right. It was only when she was apart from him that she began to worry, with Penny, whether she even knew any more where reality ended and make believe began.

She swallowed hard and forced herself to meet her friend's eyes in the mirror. She said, "I know I've let you down lately, and I'm sorry. It won't be for much longer, then everything will be back to normal. I promise."

Penny didn't look convinced, but she forced a weak smile. "Sure, Allison. Just—be careful, okay?"

As hard as she tried, Allison could not get Penny's words out of her head, and she tried not to resent her friend for that. When she had accepted the invitation the luncheon had seemed harmless enough, and

Stone's mother seemed to think it was a good idea. But maybe she *was* carrying the fantasy too far. Maybe she was only setting herself up for a painful fall.

Among the six women who met Allison for lunch at the cheerful little outdoor café, she knew only one, besides Stella. That one was Carolyn, but everyone else seemed to be perfectly nice. She could have been friends with all of them, but it did not help her mood any to realize that they all had, at one time or another, been intimate with Stone.

"We're like a big sorority," Julia, a chic-looking brunette, said with a laugh. "'Women who've loved Stone Harrison.'"

"Oh, stop it," protested someone else. "You're going to give Allison a horrible impression. It's not—" she hastened to assure Allison "—that we've all slept with him—that would be tacky beyond belief, wouldn't it? And then inviting you to lunch to compare notes?" She giggled. "No, it's just that Stone is so terribly easy to fall in love with, isn't he? Simply impossible not to adore."

Stone's mother, signaling the waiter for another Bloody Mary, suggested they might change the subject, but Allison got to spend the rest of the meal wondering just exactly which of the interesting, articulate, beautiful women displayed before her had once been Stone's lovers.

She gave her usual love-at-first-sight story when questioned on how they met, but it seemed to lack its customary sparkle. No one seemed to notice, however, or find it the least bit unusual.

"Well, I've got to say you could have knocked me over with a feather when I heard," admitted one woman, picking delicately at a fruit salad. "But I must say if ever I had imagined Stone taking the plunge it would be just like that—love at first sight, all passion and thunder, no questions asked. The only thing I find hard to believe is that he didn't sweep you away to Las Vegas that very night for the ceremony!"

Allison managed a tight smile. "I'm a bit more traditional than that."

"Did you say the wedding was the middle of November?" This was from Carolyn. "And you haven't sent out the invitations yet?"

This, as always, was where the fantasy faltered. In her mind there were horse-drawn carriages and white ribbons, a candlelit cathedral and hundreds of beautifully dressed, beatifically beaming guests. But she was forced to say, dropping her eyes, "We decided on a small ceremony. Just family."

There was a surprised, and somewhat disappointed, silence. Then, "Well, you must let us know where you're registered, at least."

Oddly no one had asked her that before. For a moment she let the fantasy expand to include exquisitely patterned silver, lace tablecloths and satin duvets, monogrammed towels and embroidered sheets.

And then Stella put in smoothly, "Don't be silly dear. They're both successful professional people with too much junk as it is. They're asking that donations be made to the Children's Hospital in honor of their marriage."

There was a round of murmured approval, and Allison cast Stella a grateful look for the save.

"Well, personally," said a honey blonde called Eileen, "I think it's just the most romantic thing I've ever heard. A whirlwind romance, a private ceremony and a honeymoon in..." She paused questioningly.

Allison smiled, meeting Stella's eyes. "Japan, we hope."

There was a chorus of excited approval, and someone else echoed, "Pure romance!"

Carolyn's smile was saccharine. "Pure theatrics, don't you mean? And that always has been Stone's strong suit. Charm and dazzle, but not much substance."

Several of the women looked shocked and disapproving, but Eileen said, "Well, there's absolutely nothing wrong with that as long as it's done right, and you've got to admit Stone has a flare. If it weren't for that six-week-itis—"

She broke off and looked at Allison, bringing her fingers to her lips in chagrin. "Oops, maybe I shouldn't have said that. You haven't been together six weeks yet have you?"

Allison lifted a puzzled eyebrow, and another woman, Diane, reached across the table to lay a hand lightly atop her arm. "Not that it applies to you, but Stone has always had this way of losing interest in a relationship at the six-week point."

"Oh." Allison forced a smile. "Yes. He told me about that."

"You see?" Diane addressed the group in general, as though it were significant. "He told her."

"And it's not as though he ever intentionally misleads a woman—you always know he's in for the short haul right from the outset."

"And he's so utterly helpless when it comes to important things. You just want to mother him to death."

"I'll tell you what used to drive me crazy. That business of only sleeping a couple of hours a night..."

"No, it was all the time he spent in that office..."

"Completely *losing* himself in his work, I mean for days at a time."

"And even when we were in the same room I wasn't always sure we were on the same planet! I really hated that. Does he do that to you, Allison?"

A moment passed before Allison registered the fact that she was being addressed. Her mind was still turning over the phrase, *you always know he's in for the short haul right from the outset,* with a peculiar, almost brutal deliberation. She had known. She had known better than any of them.

She managed a vague smile, and told the simple truth. "Actually, no. He never does."

"That proves it then. You've got to be his soul mate."

"Or he could just be going through a phase."

"Honestly, Carolyn, if we painted stripes on your back and gave you whiskers you wouldn't have to meow quite so loudly to get attention."

Allison thought, *You always know he's in for the short haul....*

The luncheon was interminable, but it finally broke up with hugs and good wishes and sincere congratulations. Allison thought, *They're really nice ladies,* but she hated them all. Not for the obvious reasons, but because she didn't belong with them, because her life had nothing to do with theirs, because she had tricked them into believing otherwise and she was getting entirely too good at that.

When the others had gone, Stella asked Allison to walk her to her car. Allison was too confused and dismayed by her own disturbed thoughts to object. Yet it was some time before Stella spoke.

"I suppose you think I'm a horrid old woman for setting this up."

Allison was startled. "I—why, no."

"And even worse for letting them go on the way they did. But I thought it was important that you hear what they had to say."

Allison didn't know how to answer that. She wasn't entirely sure she understood what the other woman meant.

Stella smiled to herself. "Well, you handled them like a lady. And you wonder why I didn't try harder to stop Gregory from going through with his crazy little scheme?" She stopped, and looked at Allison. "My dear, you are a treasure. In less than a month you have turned my son into someone I'm pleased to say I barely recognize. You've gotten him out of that mausoleum of an office and into the sunlight. You've turned his apartment into a home. And perhaps most important of all, you've managed to make him be considerate of someone besides himself for almost a month now and that in itself is a miracle. But you've made one mistake, haven't you?" She raised her hand and patted Allison's cheek softly, her eyes full of sympathy. "You've fallen in love with him."

It was, of course, as simple as that. Allison did not know why it should be so easy to admit to Stone's mother, what she had until this moment been unable to admit to herself. Nor could she explain why the kind concern in this woman's eyes should affect her more deeply than the anxiety expressed by her best friend had done. But she looked at Stella, and she found it very easy to nod.

"Yes," she said. "I suppose I have. But then, as someone said..." She smiled, and made a vague gesture back toward the restaurant. "It's easy to do."

Stella released a small sigh. "I wish I could say I'm sorry. I don't want you to be hurt. But, my dear, you have been so good for him. Dare I hope..?"

It took all of Allison's courage to hold the smile in place. She took the other woman's hand and squeezed it gently. "Don't worry about me," she said. "I know it may be hard to believe, but I do know what I'm doing. It's only for a couple of weeks more, and then..."

Anxiety darkened Stella's eyes. "And then?"

That was the trouble of course. She did not know. No one knew. But she managed another smile and gave the only answer she could. "And then," she said, "I won't be sorry."

Stone was amazed at how much his life had improved since Allison had come into it. He had always considered himself a fairly contented man, but he supposed this was a perfect example of having never known what he had missed. He liked being part of a couple. He liked being able to say, "Let me check with Allison on that"—and then actually doing it. He liked looking at her picture on his desk. He liked calling her in the middle of the day for no reason at all, and he liked having someone to come home to at night. He liked *sharing* things with her. He had never been able to do that before.

Looking back he saw the other women who had passed through his life as casual acquaintances at best. The relationships he had tried to form with them had been chores rather than privileges. But with Allison everything was different. He couldn't understand why he had never thought of becoming engaged before.

And there was more of course. He never tired of making love with her. There were times when he felt that what they shared was more than pleasure, when it seemed that even the fibers of her skin were interwoven with his. Whole days would pass when he couldn't get the taste of her, the smell of her, the *feel* of her out of his head, and that frightened him even as it thrilled him. He had never known that feeling with a woman before, that obsession, that sense of connection, and even though he didn't understand why it should be he couldn't deny it. It was enough that it simply was.

It didn't occur to him that the time would come, and in the not-too-very-distant future, when it all would end.

He liked doing things for her. He liked the way her eyes lit up when he surprised her with a nosegay of flowers from a street vendor or a box of chocolates from a specialty shop he passed on his way home or even when he remembered to bring the wine for dinner. He began to understand why things such as that were important to a woman. None of it had ever seemed important before. But to hear Allison laugh with pleasure or gasp with surprise, to see her eyes soften with tenderness or grow misty with sentiment... those things were important. And more and more he was discovering that his most contented hours were spent planning ways to bring her pleasure.

They had planned to meet at his place for dinner and he was waiting for her when she came in. He could tell immediately something was troubling her.

"Don't tell me," he said, dropping a kiss atop her slightly rumpled hair. "You had lunch with my mother."

Long before Allison reached Stone's house the courage she had displayed before his mother had faded. The brave display of savoir faire had given way to self-recriminations. Penny was right; Stella was right. Allison was a fool to let this go on. She had given her heart to a man who not only did not recognize the gift but wouldn't know what to do with it if he did. She had let a game of make believe get out of hand and she deserved to be hurt. She was crazy if she didn't put a stop to it right now.

But she walked into Stone's house and she didn't feel crazy at all; she knew exactly why she let it go on: because of moments like this. She *hadn't* told him about the luncheon, despite what she had led Penny to believe, and he had guessed anyway. And because she felt absolutely no compunction about replying, "Your mother and six of your old girlfriends."

He stifled a groan and put his arm around her shoulders, leading her into the living room. "You see, that's what I don't understand about women. Why would you want to do that to yourself?"

Allison leaned her head gratefully against his shoulders. "It was kind of interesting, actually. They all think you're adorable, by the way."

"Well, naturally." But then he placed his hands on her shoulders and turned her to face him. His expression was serious. "Allison," he said, "It was never like this with any of them. With every other woman I've known simply having a relationship has been exhausting, a list of things to do that I never got right...but with you it's easy. With you it's differ-

ent. I don't know why, but from the very first minute
everything we've had together has been perfect, and
it's felt like the most natural thing in the world."

Allison smiled, and looped her arms around his
neck and she knew then why she loved him, why it was
impossible *not* to love him. Because with him it was
easy, and because she really did not understand why.

"Stone," she said gently. "Don't you see? The reason this relationship is so easy for you is that you made
it up. Because you're playing a role, bringing a fantasy to life, and that's what you do best."

The flicker of disturbance that crossed his eyes
might have been the shadow of denial, or even disappointment. For a moment her heart caught, grasping
for a hope she had not, until that moment, even
known existed.

And then he smiled, and dropped a light kiss atop
her hair. "You're probably right," he said easily.

And almost before the bitter taste of an inexplica-
ble sadness could register in her throat, he grasped her
hand and tugged her toward the stairs. "Come on,"
he said. "I want to show you something."

His enthusiasm, as always, was contagious, and she
let him pull her up the stairs. Outside the closed guest
room door he stopped, and commanded, "Close your
eyes."

"Oh, Stone, really..." But she did, repressing a
smile of childlike anticipation. She heard him open the
door and, with one hand covering her eyes and the
other holding her arm, he guided her over the thresh-
old.

The first thing she noticed was the smell—rich, romantic, tantalizing—the kind of smell she could almost taste. Oven-warm bread and dark red wine and

garlic, and beneath that other smells, indefinable smells, such as warm rain on paving stones and ancient mosses and wide, slow-moving water. In the distance, far removed, were the muted sounds of traffic, and occasionally a snatch of music drifted out from a distant bistro. Even before Stone removed his hand and said softly, "Open your eyes," she knew where they were.

A rooftop in Paris. The wall behind them was decorated with movie posters and French graffiti. Directly before them was a table decorated with a red-checked cloth and set for two. It was from there that many of the most enticing odors emanated. And on three sides the city at dusk was spread before them— the Seine lapping the bank beneath them, stars just beginning to wink above them, traffic lights and streetlights and neon lights weaving a colorful pattern beyond, and the familiar shape of the Arc de Triomphe and, very far in the distance, the Eiffel Tower. A warm breeze ruffled the tablecloth and brushed across Allison's legs, bringing more river smells and dusk smells and alley smells, transporting her in an instant out of the world she knew and into a place she had only dreamed about before.

"I can't give you Paris," Stone said. "At least not right now. But I thought this might do for the time being."

For a moment her heart was so swollen with emotion that it filled her chest and choked off her breath. She couldn't speak. Then she turned to him, feeling the glow of love and wonder fill every fiber of her being. "Oh, Stone," she whispered. And, taking his face in her hands, she kissed him.

The succulent feast that awaited them was forgotten as the familiar breath-robbing passion swelled between them. The strength left Allison's legs and she sank to the floor, bringing Stone with her. And though the floor beneath them was plush carpet, rather than the cold concrete of a Paris rooftop, Allison barely noticed. The illusion was not diminished, for they made their own magic.

She thrust her hands beneath his sweater and pushed it up and over his head, tracing the familiar lines of his firm, lean chest, tasting its texture with her tongue. She loved the quickening of his breath, the speeding of his heart, the tightening of his hands upon her waist that signaled his reaction to her. But when he would have drawn her close to him she stopped and, with a gentle pressure of her hands upon his chest, urged him to lie back on the floor.

She sat astride his thighs, watching the light in his eyes as she shrugged out of her suit jacket, tugged off her scarf, slowly unbuttoned her blouse. His hands stroked the curve of her thighs, and his eyes were a riot of lights and darks. Playfully she drew the silk scarf over his bare chest, across his throat and heard his muffled throaty chuckle as she dropped it over his face.

"You are a wicked woman," he said. He removed the scarf to reveal eyes that were dancing with appreciation and desire. "And beautiful." He draped the scarf around her neck again. "And too good to be true..." With a gentle pressure on the ends of the scarf he drew her face down to his. He covered her mouth with his own.

As always when they made love, she was immersed in him, drowned in sensation, completely lost. He pushed her shirt down over her arms and unfastened her bra, baring her breasts. His hands caressed her back with long, firm strokes, and dizzy, fevered pleasure spun through her as he took her nipple in his mouth, drawing gently. She found the clasp of his trousers and tugged it open, then the zipper. She felt his sharp intake of breath against her skin as her fingers slipped inside, cupping and caressing his manhood. His pleasure went through her in waves of delight as intense as though they had been her own.

With her hands and mouth she explored the strong planes and lean muscled lines of a body she knew as well as she knew her own and yet, every time she touched him, the sensation was as wondrous, and as exciting, as if it were the first. When she took him inside her it was as if she were coming home. It was the only time she ever felt complete. If there was a thread of desperation in the way she reached for him it was only because she missed him a little more each time they were apart. If there was a touch of frantic longing in her kisses it was only because she knew their time together grew shorter with every day. And if she clung to him long after the point of physical satiation it was only because she knew how soon the time would come when she must let him go forever, and the aching emptiness that was inside her wouldn't completely go away. All she wanted was for this moment to last. All she needed was for it to be real.

When at last they lay entwined and exhausted beneath the darkening Paris sky, Stone dropped gentle kisses on her fevered face and Allison tried to make her arms relax their fierce grip around him. *I won't be sorry,* she told herself. *I won't.* He had given her Paris, and even though it was only an illusion, she would always love him for that.

She turned in his arms, making herself release him, opening her eyes. He smiled down at her, gentle and adoring. "I wish you could see," he said softly, "how beautiful you look to me now."

Allison lifted her hand, and touched his face. No one could have looked more beautiful than he did to her. His hair was damp, his face flushed and his eyes held the secrets of the universe. She loved him. More than anything in the world she wanted to tell him so.

But she smiled, and said instead, "Where did you get the food?"

His eyes crinkled. "I called a caterer. I knew it wouldn't be as good as the dinner you would have fixed, but sometimes you have to take second best."

"Paris beneath the stars," she murmured. "I like your idea of second best."

She knew of course that the holographic program was one he had designed for the Heroshito project. She also knew the enormous amount of effort and expense that had been required to move the cumbersome projection equipment and transform this room to his design specifications. This evening had not been accomplished on an impulse, or a careless whim. She wondered if he had ever done anything such as this for any other woman and found herself hoping desperately that he had not. Or if he had, that she would never, ever find out about it.

And in one of those wondrous moments of perfect communication where it seemed he almost read her mind, he said softly, "I never wanted to share this with anyone else before."

"Paris?"

"Paris, Celiton Three . . . my dreams."

She smiled tremulously, loving him. With the tip of her finger she traced the shape of his lips. Her voice was touched with the wonder of slow understanding as she said, "You never see the wires, do you? You design the illusion, you know every working part, but when the time comes to spin the fantasy . . . you don't see the wires. You believe it."

He caught her hand and pressed it to his lips, smiling. "Of course. Don't you?"

And that, of course, was the trouble. Allison did believe it. She had from the beginning.

Ten

—

Even though Allison knew the time line and expected the inevitable, she was not prepared for how quickly the next two weeks went by. She and Stone worked together like a well-oiled machine in preparation for the final presentation, and when she looked back she would find that those were among the happiest days she had ever spent—working with him, sharing ideas with him and being, for however brief a time, part of his world.

The three members of the Heroshito group who would be responsible for the final assignment of the contract arrived with their wives for a week of meetings and interviews. Two were Japanese, one was British, and with Mark, the ever-present liaison, they made a colorful and eclectic group.

Allison had carefully arranged Stone's schedule so that the mornings were clear for meetings and technical demonstrations and the afternoons were free for leisure entertainment, often ending with dinner or a show. Because family values seemed to be important to the Heroshito people she assumed that a demonstration of the same values on Stone's part—by arranging activities that brought them all together for at least part of the day—would be appropriate, and she was right. A little research had revealed that this was the first trip to Southern California for two of the men, and for all of the wives, and she assumed—again correctly—that they would want to treat the trip in part as if it was a working vacation. She arranged excursions to the beach, popular tourist spots, trendy restaurants—exactly the things she would want to see if she were visiting the city for the first time—but carefully avoided the most popular theme parks and studio tours, because she did not want anything to compete with or detract from Stone's grand presentation on the final night.

While Stone was busy in negotiations, Allison took charge of the wives, taking them shopping on Rodeo Drive, or "stargazing" in the Polo Lounge, or simply lounging by the pool in true California style. She found the Japanese women to be somewhat more demure than she was accustomed to, but they made no attempt to curb her American opinions or disapprove of her style. She found their customs and culture even as Westernized as it had become, fascinating, and their description of their homeland enchanting. The British woman, who had a unique sense of humor, immediately made a friend of Allison and admitted that it was Japan she missed when she traveled with her husband, not Britain. And Allison found herself yearning to see that ancient land of wonder and beauty—forgetting, for a time, that it was highly unlikely that she ever would.

She was aware that she was under just as much scrutiny as Stone was, and that it was part of her job to pass every test—but she never once thought of it as a job, or even a test. Though the other wives' interview technique was very subtle, Allison answered each question honestly and straightforwardly. When Sarah told her privately that the other women thought she was wonderful, Allison was as thrilled as if it really mattered—as if somewhere in her future there was a gold band, a trip to Japan, a proud successful husband who relied on her advice and needed her by his side.

Had the week been less frantic, less busy and intense, she might very well have cried herself to sleep every night for all she was about to lose. As it was, both she and Stone were too exhausted each night to do more than fall into each other's arms and sleep. Very often Allison dreamed about Japan. By then she realized just how important it was not to let herself see the wires: everything depended on her believing the fantasy. And by then, of course, she had no choice. She loved Stone too much not to believe it.

The theme of the park Stone had designed was "Other Worlds." The premise was that the visitor could be transported to the most thrilling and unique places on earth—and elsewhere—without ever leaving his own land. From the mystery and adventure of an undersea cavern to the excitement of an African jungle or the enigma of a Mayan pyramid; from the world's most exotic capitals to the farthest reaches of outer space. A combination of sights, sounds, tex-

tures and smells brought the far away home, made the
unimaginable real, formed the basis for thrilling rides
and unforgettable adventures. The prototype would be
built, of course, in Japan, but plans were underway
for six more parks of similar scope and theme to be
built around the world. For Stone it was a dream come
true.

The group had been reviewing plans, watching
videotapes, discussing numbers, schedules and specifications all week. Of course they had personally in-
spected other examples of Stone's work, but to that
point had seen none of the prototypes for the new
park. Allison planned to center the unveiling around
a "movable feast" that began with a breathtaking ride
to Celiton Three for the first course, moved to a tree
house in the jungle for the salad and ended in a café in
Paris with dessert and coffee. The evening brought out
the child in even the most staid of the visitors. Even as
they reached Celiton Three they were laughing and
exclaiming with delight. By the main course the thin
but distinct barrier of formality that had been present
all week had dissolved completely. By dessert they
were all chatting and exchanging memories as if they
were old friends.

Allison knew that all the work and worry was worth
it when she heard Mark exclaim under his breath to
Stone, "Inspired! Absolutely brilliant! The fanciest ad
agency on Madison Avenue couldn't have come up
with a better presentation. No wonder they call you a
genius!"

And she thought her heart would burst with pride
when Stone replied easily, "It was Allison's idea. In
fact, you have her to thank for the entire evening, and
I'm forced to agree—it was inspired." He met her eyes

across the table and smiled. With Paris spread out before them and candlelight flickering between them, they shared more than a moment. They shared memories.

He lifted his glass, his eyes sparkling and never leaving hers. "Ladies, gentlemen—please. A toast to my bride—the best part of Stonewall Enterprises."

The clamor of "Hear, hear!" and clinking glasses faded around Allison, because she was lost in Stone's eyes. That was the best moment of the evening. Perhaps the best moment of her life.

It was even better than the next, in which Mark tapped his glass with his spoon for attention. "Another toast, then." He raised his glass. "To Stone and Allison—a beautiful couple, a perfect team and the newest members, however temporary, of the Heroshito family."

Glass clinked, faces beamed. Stone sat very still. So did Allison. "Congratulations, Stone." Mark smiled. "I told you a decision would be made tomorrow but after what we've seen tonight there isn't much left to discuss. Welcome aboard." He turned to Allison and raised his glass again. "Both of you."

They managed to contain themselves until they reached home. Stone turned on the lamp, and Allison closed the door. They looked at each other across the room. They burst into simultaneous laughter.

With a whoop of victory Stone ran to Allison and swept her up, whirling her around, raining kisses on her face. "We did it! By God, we did it! It's over...we pulled it off...we did it!"

"*You* did it! I knew you would, there was never any doubt. Stone, you were brilliant!"

"You were brilliant! They loved you! My God, Allison, tonight was incredible, even *I* didn't know it could be that good! Are we great or what?"

And then he kissed her, whirling her around and around, and she kissed him back, laughing and gasping through her dizziness, hugging him.

When he set her down they leaned against each other, steadying themselves, still laughing, holding each other while the world steadied and reality slowly sank in. Only reality for Allison was quite different from what it was for Stone.

She could see the wonder form in his eyes as the truth settled in by stages. "I did it," he said slowly. "I got the contract. I can't believe it. I've wanted it for so long...Allison, do you realize what this means?"

"It means," she replied, caressing the back of his neck in a single tender gesture, "that you are going to be one famous engineer, and hundreds of thousands—millions—of people are going to have their dreams come true. Could you ask for better?"

"No." His hands tightened on her waist, and he drew her toward him. "I couldn't have done it without you."

She stopped him with a hand planted gently but firmly in the center of his chest. She forced a brittle smile. "Hey. That's what I get paid for, remember?"

He stared at her. Confusion replaced the happiness in his eyes. "Allison..."

"Stone, I'm so proud of you," she said earnestly. "Of you, of us, of what we've done together...of what you're going to do. You're the best. You deserve this. But..." Gently she disentangled herself. "I only signed on for the short-term, remember? And it's over now."

"I don't understand." His voice was hoarse, his eyes searched hers as though hoping for some sign that would contradict her words. "What we've had... Allison, it was more than just a job. For God's sake, what are you saying?"

She cupped his cheek gently with her hand. "I know it was," she said softly. "And I've enjoyed every minute of it. But we both knew it was just a game, didn't we? It was never meant to last."

He dropped his eyes. Slowly he let his hands fall from her waist. "Yes," he said heavily, after a time. "I suppose so."

It was another moment before Allison could make her voice strong enough to continue. "You're a six-week guy, Stone. And my time was up yesterday."

He released a long, slow breath. Half turning from her, he thrust his fingers through his hair. "You're right. I just—I never thought about the future before. I never thought about it ending."

And Allison said bleakly, "Maybe that's the trouble."

Neither one of them seemed to know what to say then. The silence went on forever, empty and desolate and weary.

Allison said, with a great effort, "I already packed my things and took them home." She wanted to smile at the surprise in his eyes, but she couldn't. He hadn't even noticed. Some things about him hadn't changed at all. "Tomorrow, or the next day, whenever the contract is signed, you can tell them we broke up, and everything will be finished. It'll work out fine."

After a long time Stone nodded. "Yeah." But his eyes looked stunned, dazed, like a man at the scene of an accident who doesn't want to believe what he sees. "Just like I planned."

Allison said, "Right."

She turned toward the door, then stopped. Tugging at the ring on her finger, she crossed the room to him. "Thanks, Stone." She forced one last smile, and placed the ring in his hand. "It was a hell of a ride."

And then quickly, while she still could, she left.

"I can't believe you did it," Penny said. Her tone was hushed with awe, yet carefully subdued, the tone of voice one uses at a funeral home or a state function. "That from the very first you planned . . . you knew you had to leave him and you actually *did* it."

Allison's living room matched the tone of Penny's voice—the drapes were drawn, unanswered mail was stacked on the corner of her desk, the telephone was on the answering machine, the gloom was dispelled only by a dim lamp in the far corner. Allison sat on the sofa with her knees drawn up, her hands wrapped around a cup of cooling tea. She said tiredly, "I knew the price of admission before I got on."

Penny sat beside her, her face lined with sympathy. "And I didn't make it any easier for you, with all my well-meaning advice. Oh, Allison, I'm so sorry. Because—you weren't just pretending to be in love with him, were you?"

Allison shook her head slowly, and managed a small, bitter smile. "There were even times . . . when I thought he wasn't pretending, either."

"I don't understand it," Penny said. "I don't understand how you could leave him when you know you still love him."

"I couldn't stand the suspense of waiting for that look on his face," Allison replied simply. "When he wakes up one morning and realizes that the game was over. That he didn't need me anymore. It would have been hard for him, then, I think to tell me it was over . . . to hurt me. This way, it was part of the script. It never got too real." She forced herself to take a sip of the tea. It tasted bitter and thick, like tears.

"And I'll tell you a secret," she added softly, staring into the teacup. "All the time I kept hoping he would stop me. If he'd just once said something, or done something . . . but he never did."

Penny put her arm around Allison's shoulders in the kind of sympathetic understanding only another woman can give, but she said nothing. There was nothing anyone could say.

This should have been the happiest time of Stone's life. He was embarking on the biggest adventure a man could have—more than just a dream come true, the culmination of a lifetime worth of pushing the limits, daring the impossible, reaching for the stars. He was only thirty-two years old and already he had reached the pinnacle of his career. Then why did it feel like such an empty victory?

He knew the answer to that, of course. Because every time a new detail for enhancement of the plans occurred to him he wanted to share it with Allison. Because he would turn to ask her something or discuss something with her and she wasn't there; because he put his hand on the phone a dozen times a day and realized he had no one to call; because he still walked into a room expecting to see her there and when she wasn't the emptiness that sank through him was colder and bleaker than anything he had ever known.

He signed the contract, but when Mark suggested they all go out to celebrate, Stone told him he and Allison had planned a private party at home, just the two of them. He couldn't bring himself to tell the facile story of the tragic breakup—which was now the truth—he had invented for the occasion. His mother knew the truth, of course, and so did Carla. His secretary hadn't spoken to him in six days, and his mother hung up the phone every time he called.

He had a month to organize his affairs, pack up his office and his household and be ready to move his entire operation to Japan. Allison would have known how to do that—what to pack and what to leave, what documents to file, how to arrange for storage, what tradespeople to hire. And at first he was angry. How dare she leave him just when he needed her most? How could she reduce what they had shared to nothing more than a job that ended on a timetable? How could she just walk out of his life this way?

But it had been just a job...hadn't it? They had both agreed on the terms from the outset. They had a great time and accomplished incredible things but from the beginning they both had known it was only make believe. He couldn't be angry with her for that.

Then he tried denial. Just because the job was over didn't mean they couldn't go on seeing each other. Just because their personal relationship was over didn't mean they couldn't still be friends. All of his ex-girlfriends were still friends. They talked on the phone, they had lunch, they laughed together...but he couldn't picture himself doing any of those things with

Allison. She wasn't like his other girlfriends, she never had been. With her it was all or nothing.

And he was left with nothing.

On the sixth day he arrived at the office late, as had become his custom recently, and Carla said, without looking up, "Your mother's waiting for you."

His step faltered with surprise. For almost a week she had managed to conduct business without uttering a word, but somehow he did not take this break in the icy silence as a good sign—any more than he could assume his mother's presence meant a thawing on the home front. It was with more than a little trepidation that he stepped into his private office and closed the door.

He smiled and went forward to greet his mother, but she averted her face and flung out a hand in a grandly theatrical gesture. "Don't bother," she commanded. "I do *not* forgive you."

Stone muttered, "Oh, for Pete's sake." He went around his desk and sat down, folding his arms across his chest in an air of resignation. "All right," he said invitingly. "Go ahead. I'm ready."

She placed her palms on his desk and leaned forward intently. "Gregory Stonewall Harrison, I have put up with a great deal from you over the years. Frogs in my teapot, indelible ink on my wallpaper, electrical appliances disembowelled and rearranged in the most obscene fashion, forgotten birthdays, unreturned phone calls, inappropriate Christmas gifts.... But this...this has gone too far. This is stupidity at its most refined. This is *incomprehensible*."

"Will you stop it?" He pushed up from his desk in a sudden explosion of temper that was as much of a surprise to him as it was to his mother. "Will everybody just stop it?'' He stalked away from her, toward the window. ''I wish somebody would explain to me what the big deal is! Why am I being treated like a criminal? It was a business deal, for God's sake! We all knew how it was going to end before we started it. And even if it hadn't been—she's the one who walked out on me, not the other way around!''

''And that,'' declared his mother with a satisfied nod, ''is the only good thing that came out of this entire fiasco. For the first time in your life someone left you before you were ready to let her go and that, in my opinion, was well worth waiting for. But *you're* the idiot who let her go!''

Stone turned around slowly, staring at her. But before he could utter a word she went on sharply, ''As for what the 'big deal' is, my fine young man—she loved you! And you needn't pretend you didn't feel the same way about her because I know you better! That girl was the best thing that ever happened to you and you played with her emotions. You strung her along, you lied to her—and then you let her go! I'm ashamed to call you my flesh and blood.''

Stone's eyes dropped to the photograph on his desk. He should have returned it, or at least put it away, but he hadn't been able to bring himself to do so. He swallowed hard, but his voice still sounded a little hoarse as he replied, ''It was just a game. We were only pretending.''

His mother looked at him scornfully. ''If you believe that, then you deserve whatever you get. As for the way you've treated that poor girl…I came to make my opinion known, and there's nothing more to be said.'' She picked up a sharp-edged letter opener from the desk and handed it to him deliberately, point up.

The look she gave him was stern and meaningful. "I will leave you alone now. I can only trust you will do the honorable thing."

She turned sharply on her heel and left.

Stone sat down behind the desk, slumping in his chair. Allison gazed back at him from the framed photograph, laughing, windblown, beautiful. He picked the picture up, and he looked at it for a very long time.

Then he picked up the telephone.

Mark's expression was stunned, wrestling with disbelief. "So... you lied. You and Allison—you never had any intention of getting married at all. You just made up the whole thing to better your chances at the contract."

Stone nodded. "It didn't seem dishonest at the time. That rule about married men seemed arbitrary and absurd and it wasn't fair that it should stand in my way when I was the best man for the job."

"Maybe so," Mark admitted reluctantly, "but..."

"Now I see their point, though," Stone went on quietly. "A married man *does* have more at stake, he does have more to care about... more to be proud of. A married man, I guess, has more of everything. What I did was wrong, any way you look at it. And I wanted you to know."

Mark drew a hand over his jaw in subdued agitation, releasing a pent-up breath. "Stone, I'm disappointed in you. Everyone will be. But—in a way I guess I can understand why you did it, and there's no getting around the fact that a contract is a contract. You've still got the job."

Stone shook his head regretfully. "No, you don't understand. The reason I came to you now is to give you notice that you might want to start reconsidering the other bids, because I really don't know if I'll be able to take the job."

Mark stared at him in outright disbelief, and Stone got to his feet.

"You see," he explained, smiling, "I never really got around to asking Allison how she felt about living in Japan."

Allison kept telling herself that two weeks' mourning was quite enough for a relationship that had never really existed at all, but as November 16—her make-believe wedding day—approached, her depression only grew worse. She didn't know why, but she kept expecting Stone to call. Everyone else called—his mother, his friends, his secretary. She let the messages pile up on the answering machine, waiting for the one voice that would change her life. But it never came.

And in her more logical moments she knew it wouldn't. She had fulfilled her part of the bargain and Stone was no doubt grateful but he was busy now, packing for the move, getting ready to open a whole new chapter in his life, embarking on a new and grand adventure—and he would do it without her. She had always known that, and it was time now for her to get on with her own life.

Recovery would have no doubt been a great deal easier if she had been able to work, if she could have immersed herself in some project that would take her mind off Stone for a good long time. Thanks to the contacts Stone had given them, the future of Party

Girls looked solid, at least until well into next year. But at the present time the only project Penny had underway was a wedding. It was a fairy-tale affair with white lace and roses, so dripping with sentiment and tradition that Penny claimed it was all she could do to keep from gagging...exactly the kind of thing that Allison, under normal circumstances, would have immersed herself in ecstatically. Presently, however, she simply was not up to dealing with someone else's dream wedding, and she found herself spending more and more time secluded in her bedroom while the world went on without her. Just as Stone was going on quite happily without her.

She made up her mind that as soon as the make-believe wedding date had passed she would pull herself together, put Stone out of her mind and get busy picking up the pieces of her life. So on November 15 she cried herself to sleep for the last time, said goodbye to what might have been with all the conviction she could muster and prepared herself to face the first day of the rest of her life with courage and fortitude.

After a troubled, sleepless night, she was awakened the next morning by the muffled blare of trumpets. She groaned and pulled a pillow over her head. The noise did not go away. Gradually she recognized the tune as the "Wedding March" and thought her partner must be trying out a new arrangement on the stereo. "For God's sake, Penny," she muttered, trying to squirm down deeper beneath the pillow.

But the music only grew louder, dragging her reluctantly and painfully from sleep, and she realized it couldn't possibly be the stereo. It sounded as though it was coming from outside—from the street right below her window, as a matter of fact.

Allison stumbled out of bed, cursing softly under her breath, and made her way to the window. She pushed back the curtain, blinking irritably in the light, then stopped, staring. Even after her eyes adjusted to the light she had to rub them twice, unable to believe what she saw, but it didn't go away.

Beneath her window was a gilded horse-drawn carriage. Two white horses tossed plumed helmets and beribboned harnesses fluttered in the breeze. The upholstery was white velvet and the spokes were wrapped in ribbons and white roses. Behind the carriage was a string of white limousines, many with the moon roofs open. To the first limousine were attached the stereo speakers that blared forth the "Wedding March," and from the others spilled a variety of gaily dressed, laughing and waving people—obviously the wedding party and guests.

Abruptly aware of how visible she was, standing at the window in her nightgown, Allison backed away, still blinking. Had Penny gone crazy? What were all those people doing here? She should have *known* better than to let Penny plan a wedding by herself....

She scrambled for her robe, opening her mouth to shout for Penny, when suddenly the door burst open and Penny strode in. Allison could do nothing but stare.

Penny was wearing a deep rose, three-quarter-length gown of petal-cut taffeta and a wide-brimmed matching organza hat—almost identical to the outfits Allison had seen on some of the ladies in the wedding party below. Her eyes were sparkling and her color was high and, most incredible of all, she carried, carefully arranged over her outstretched arms, an ivory satin wedding gown.

Allison found her voice, though it was barely a hoarse gasp. "Penny, what in the world—"

But then Stella Blake swept through the door in a pink lace suit and incredible feathered hat, carrying what must have been nine yards of wedding veil across her arms. As Allison watched, stunned with incredulity, the two women carefully laid both garments across the rumpled bed. And just when Allison had almost recovered her breath, she looked up and saw Stone.

He was wearing a cutaway and striped cravat, holding a top hat in his hand. He was so devastatingly handsome that the mere sight of him would have taken anyone's breath away, even if it hadn't been for the shock of his unexpected appearance in Allison's bedroom. His face was sober and composed, his eyes heartbreakingly tender and alive with that wondrous, secret light she knew so well as his gaze moved over her. That's when Allison decided she must still be sleeping, safely dreaming in her own bed, and she hoped she never woke up.

Stella Blake snatched a pillow from the bed and tossed it on the floor at Allison's feet. "Well, hurry up," she commanded. "We've only got twenty minutes to get to the church and we still have to make the bride beautiful."

Stone cast his mother an impatient look. "I might have better luck," he told her, "if she didn't have to be reminded right now who her mother-in-law is going to be."

And Penny tugged at Stella's arm. "Maybe we'd better leave them alone," she urged softly. The look she tossed Allison was sparkling and excited as she lead Stella, who looked highly affronted, from the room.

Allison and Stone were alone, and she knew it was no dream.

For the longest time they simply looked at each other. The sound of their heartbeats seemed to fill the room. Then Stone gestured toward the window, where the sound of trumpets still filled the air. A smile flicked across his lips but his eyes never left hers, and his eyes were hungry. "Special effects are my business," he reminded her. "I hope you don't mind."

She couldn't answer. She could only stand and drink him in, drowning in him, wanting it never to end.

He said, "I wanted to give you your fantasy, Allison. White horses, lace and satin, white roses...maybe it would have been better if you'd done it all yourself, but I wanted to surprise you. I just hope..." His eyes moved anxiously over her face. "That you don't mind if I'm part of your fantasy."

Stone came forward, and took both of her hands in his. He dropped to one knee on the pillow at her feet. Looking up at her, he said softly, "It was love at first sight. I never thought it could happen to me but it did. Everything about you went right through me, like someone threw a spear into my soul, and it stopped me cold. You set my soul on fire, you crawled inside my skin, you were the beginning and the ending of everything I had ever known. Together, we are magic, and I can't see the future without you in it."

He reached into his pocket and took something out. Holding her left hand in his, he slipped the ring on her finger. "Allison, will you marry me? Please."

Through a blur of misty, hot tears, Allison looked down at her hand, spreading her fingers. The fake di-

amond winked and flashed in the sunlight, and it was
the most beautiful thing she had ever seen. "Oh,
Stone," she whispered. "My zircon."

"Actually," he said, and a brief look of guilt
crossed his face. "I looked for a zircon, but I couldn't
find one that looked good enough for you to wear. I'm
afraid I lied to you about the ring, Allison." He got to
his feet, still holding her hand. "It's real. It always
was."

A laugh of sheer joy escaped her even as the tears at
last brimmed over. She threw her arms around him,
holding him tightly, losing herself in the strength of his
returned embrace. "Yes," she agreed, squeezing her
eyes closed against the happiness that threatened to
overwhelm her. "It always was."

* * * * *

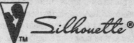

Take 4 bestselling love stories FREE

Plus get a FREE surprise gift!

In the spirit of Christmas, Silhouette invites you to share the joy of the holiday season.

Experience the beauty of Yuletide romance with Silhouette Christmas Stories 1992—a collection of heartwarming stories by favorite Silhouette authors.

JONI'S MAGIC by Mary Lynn Baxter
HEARTS OF HOPE by Sondra Stanford
THE NIGHT SANTA CLAUS RETURNED by Marie Ferrarella
BASKET OF LOVE by Jeanne Stephens

This Christmas you can also receive a FREE keepsake Christmas ornament. Look for details in all November and December Silhouette books.

Also available this year are three popular early editions of Silhouette Christmas Stories—1986, 1987 and 1988. Look for these and you'll be well on your way to a complete collection of the best in holiday romance.

Share in the celebration—with Silhouette's
Christmas gift of love.

SX92

It's Opening Night in October—
and you're invited!
Take a look at romance with a
brand-new twist, as the stars
of tomorrow make their
debut today!
It's LOVE:
an age-old story—
now, with
*WORLD PREMIERE
APPEARANCES* by:

Patricia Thayer—Silhouette Romance #895
JUST MAGGIE—Meet the Texas rancher who wins this pretty
teacher's heart…and lose your own heart, too!

Anne Marie Winston—Silhouette Desire #742
BEST KEPT SECRETS—Join old lovers reunited and see what
secret wonders have been hiding…beneath the flames!

Sierra Rydell—Silhouette Special Edition #772
ON MIDDLE GROUND—Drift toward Twilight, Alaska, with this
widowed mother and collide—heart first—into body heat
enough to melt the frozen tundra!

Kate Carlton—Silhouette Intimate Moments #454
KIDNAPPED!—Dare to look on as a timid wallflower blos-
soms and falls in fearless love—with her gruff, mysterious
kidnapper!

**Don't miss the classics of tomorrow—
premiering today—only from**

PREM

TAKE A WALK ON THE DARK SIDE OF LOVE

October is the shivery season, when chill winds blow and shadows walk the night. Come along with us into a haunting world where love and danger go hand in hand, where passions will thrill you and dangers will chill you. Come with us to

SILHOUETTE
Shadows™

In this newest short story collection from Sihouette Books, three of your favorite authors tell tales just perfect for a spooky autumn night. Let Anne Stuart introduce you to "The Monster in the Closet," Helen R. Myers bewitch you with "Seawitch," and Heather Graham Pozzessere entice you with "Wilde Imaginings."

Silhouette Shadows™
Haunting a store near you this October.

Silhouette®